going anywhere

going anywhere

Stories

david armstrong

Leapfrog Press
Fredonia, New York

Published in 2014 in the United States by
Leapfrog Press LLC
PO Box 505
Fredonia, NY 14063
www.leapfrogpress.com

Printed in the United States of America

Distributed in the United States by
Consortium Book Sales and Distribution
St. Paul, Minnesota 55114
www.cbsd.com

First Edition

Author photo courtesy of Kevin Dossinger

Library of Congress Cataloging-in-Publication Data

Armstrong, David M., 1977-
[Short stories. Selections]
Going anywhere : stories / David Armstrong. -- First edition.
pages cm
ISBN 978-1-935248-61-3 (pbk. : alk. paper)
I. Title.
PS3601.R5748A6 2014
813'.6--dc23
2014029912

For M, who is my home,
and P, who is still a part of it

contents

acknowledgments

Writing is like chasing ghosts with a butterfly net. It's a feeble attempt to capture something ephemeral and, dare I say it, magical—something made up of memory and meaning—using only that blunt instrument, the written word. In thanking those who need thanking, I'm certain I'll be just as imperfect and forgetful as in all my endeavors. There are many beyond the few mentioned here who had a hand in supporting me and creating this book. For their emotional and intellectual nourishment, I'm forever grateful. That said, thank you to my mother and father, Don and Karen Armstrong. Thank you also to Drew and Katie Armstrong, Jenny Moore, Rosemary Yates, Daniel Armstrong, Richard Wiley, Maile Chapman, Doug Unger, Carol Harter, Damien and Ashley Cowger, Dustin Faulstick, Jolynn Baldwin, Colby Gillette, David Ballenger, Kyle Hildebrandt, Darrell Spencer, Joan Connor, Eric and Kristin LeMay, Darlene and John Unrue, Loreen L. Giese, Andrew Malan Milward, Paul Sacksteder, Michael Van Auken, and James Miranda. For their editorial support, thank you to Lev Raphael, Lisa Graziano, Chris Offutt, Matt Bell, Amelia Gray, Amber Sparks, Tom Dibblee, Michael Kardos, Bryan Tomasovich, Matt Sailor, and Kellen Shaver. Also a special thanks to a woman whose commanding knowledge of the mechanics of language I didn't fully appreciate until my adult life—Mary Jean Rieder, my high school Latin teacher. And finally, a thanks beyond thanks to my wife, Melinda, who is everything and everything and more than everything always.

take care

She said she was going anywhere.

I told her that was a long way from here, which was no-where.

She didn't laugh.

I'd found her shivering near the highway, crouched against the wide, rust-addled post of the truckstop sign, the sign's heavy yellow letters hollowing out a nimbus in the night sky overhead: *A&K Aero-Stop, Heat and Electrical Hook-up, Shower and Eats.* I'd been turning over the miles for six days, crisscrossing the country in long, jagged sojourns of sleepless hours, downing coffee and Red Bulls, yellow-bees, a few dud reds a waitress sold me—I'd even foil-burned a dull shard of meth, which tweaked me for two days and tore out my guts the whole time—in hopes of losing whatever it was was chasing me.

She was nineteen if a day, a white girl with dreads, wearing a homemade sleeveless top and a corduroy skirt. She slid into my car silently and without looking me in the eye. Then we were off again, down the hueless highway somewhere in the middle flat dark of Ohio in my old Lincoln Continental with broken number-locks on the doors and a flaking skin of topcoat dull on the hood under moonlight. The car was an easy ride, a boat-swell bounce to the air-shocks, and we were fifteen miles away from that truckstop doing eighty, the radio low with some sad song I couldn't place from my college days, when she finally spoke again.

"I'm Trese," she said.

"Terese?"

"Trese. One syllable."

"Doug."

"Sex?" she said.

"I don't need that. It's not an exchange." I didn't want it to sound like a rejection and tried to make her feel pretty by gesturing to her bare shoulder, her face. "I just don't."

"I'm not making any value judgments," she said. "It's expected sometimes. I understand." She crossed her arms and stared into the window, her face making a green reflection in the glass, lit up by the glow from the radio numbers.

"Where are you headed?" she said. She didn't look at me, just looked out into the dry black fields rushing by. "You asked me. So where are *you* going?"

"Anywhere," I said. I tapped a rimshot on the steering wheel.

"Seriously."

"Usually hitchhikers are just happy for a ride."

"You make me nervous. I ask questions."

"I make you nervous?"

"Going to see family?" she said.

"Going away from family, then back maybe, would be closer to it."

"You look respectable, is all I mean. Middle-age. Haircut. Maybe you need a shower. But you look like you belong somewhere."

"I'm a domesticated dog, is what you mean."

"Just not like a trucker. Not a traveler."

I was wearing khaki pants, but only because my jeans

had been stained. I'd bought the button-up shirt at a Sears in Billings, Montana. I'd never been to a more depressing place than the Sears in Billings, Montana.

"And yet I make you nervous," I said.

"You give off a creep vibe."

"Bit abrupt for somebody I could leave in the middle of a cow pasture."

"Cow pastures I can handle," she said. "Cow pastures are a piece of cake. It's people that get you. It's why I ask up front. A guy either wants it or he doesn't. If he wants it, we get it over with or make a deal. It's civil. The one thing I can't take is a guy getting creepy, you know?"

"And I'm already that guy."

"The guys who say no, those are normally the creepy ones. They go, I'm married. They show a ring. Then they lay a hand on your thigh. Inch up there with a pinky finger. God, if you want to fuck, just fuck, right? I'm not high and mighty. I won't tattle."

"You seem to have a lot of experience."

She tightened her arms under her breasts. She had two piercings in her left ear, one in the lobe and one in the cartilage, and a small silver chain connected them.

"I'm going to Raleigh," I said.

"Fuck North Carolina." She'd gone sour. I'd given off some vibe, sent little waves of nausea, little roaches of unease, scurrying up her legs and spine.

"I'm terrible at hiding things," I said. "I've been driving for days. Just driving. This discomfort you feel. You're right to feel it. You're not right about why. But you're right."

"If I ask you to pull over, you better pull over," she said.

"But you're not asking me to pull over."

She tugged at the seatbelt like a pair of too-tight pants, pressed on the old motorized seat so it reclined with a groan. She rolled half on her side away from me. "Don't even try to touch me," she said. "You had your chance."

We drove in the murky, sweet quiet, maybe five minutes or an hour. Time was losing its consistency. I couldn't tell when I'd slept last. The days and evenings had overlapped slowly, like breaking waves rolling and being sucked under themselves.

I drove and I waited until I heard her snoring lightly. It reminded me of a little kid. Then I started talking as quietly as I could.

"I should practice this," I said. "Read it to somebody." I felt for the piece of paper I'd shoved into my pocket a hundred times, took it out, and laid it across the wheel. The words, written in pencil, were indiscernible in the dark, but I could feel them sitting there, testing the air in front of me with their weight, lifting off the page and gathering physical shape.

I imagined what was to come, the lectern, the respectable expressions of all those sad faces, the bend at the edges of their lips, the brows smartly sober or upright in what remained of their bewilderment. I imagined the strange formality of them having to take their seats, as if they were at any other gathering, a lecture or a string quartet recital, and then the preacher would speak and read and lead them in the singing and gently extend his arm to me because I said I'd do it. I wanted to get it right.

I would say what a shock it was. I would want to tell them the details about my wife Jessica and I going to Key West for a week. I'd want them to know that our daughter Anna would have been twenty-one in the fall. She was home alone. I'd want them to know that the world has no meaning, that Anna had fallen, hit her head on the bottom step of the staircase and died. That maybe if someone finds you there, lying like that, in time, you are taken to a hospital and the swelling in your brain is released in a touch-and-go procedure by neurological surgeons, but you don't die. You certainly don't do that. I'd want people to know that you should never give up your children. Never leave them for a week to go to Key West. I'd want those people staring up at me to know it was all my fault because, while I know you can't always be there, I could have been.

take care

Except these aren't the words on the page. Some of the words are like this, but they aren't clear. They're jumbled scraps of memory jotted down outside of Raleigh, then in Mississippi and in Dallas before I turned north for Colorado and Wyoming and the vastness of everything, and the wide horizon turned the world to a sun-soaked blur until I turned back east, toward North Carolina, where our home with its multi-toned brick facade sits on a street where elms have been planted in the grass-green median, and there are women there who bury the tulip bulbs in the winter so that they bloom in the spring, and then there is Jessica, and she's in the kitchen and there is nothing to say but this. Our child is gone. Our everything is lost.

The autopsy and inquest have delayed the funeral, and if I drive straight through I'll be back in time. My phone went dead a long while back, but I called from a rest stop with a calling card and heard my brother Tom's voice, and Tom didn't make me speak, just said they were going ahead with the burial and he hoped I'd be there. He said, Take care of yourself.

And now the words are written in front of me on the steering wheel, and even though I can't see them, I know them.

"A box turtle in the leaves," I say. This I wrote in the upper left-hand corner. I wrote it first and it's the shakiest because I rested the paper on my thigh as I drove.

"The cost of her trumpet.

"The shallow end of the pool.

"A surprise in the dryer.

"Pie."

Because all of them are fragments. Little lost leaves of memory touching down to earth, and I'm scooping them up and trying to give them weight, trying to find a way of putting them into the formal structures that will mean something to others.

"Prom hairstyles.

"Math is a girl's best friend."

Prompts. While driving I had tried, in a moment of exhaustion, to write that one down, about the time I'd seen her so happy about the math scores for the AP test. I did it a few days ago in the car, trying to put it to paper while still holding my coffee, and I turned the cup over like an idiot, forgetting it was even in my hand, and dumping it all over my lap. And that was in Montana, and that was the one about math.

I'm reading the prompts out loud, and I'm not seeing them on the page because I know they're there.

"Crickets for the science fair.

"Jake.

"Our car accident.

"The misspelled banner.

"Teething. Fever.

And it all feels too light.

"Did you say something?" Trese is awake, and again I don't know how long it's been.

"I was reading," I say. I put the paper away some time ago, tucked it back into my pocket.

"Seems dangerous."

"No more dangerous than most things."

"Where are we?"

"We just crossed over into West Virginia."

"Oh. So what's that over there?" She points at some lights in the distance. A few blips scattered across a black dip in the land. We climb a grade in the highway and the lights take shape as a series of buildings cast against a low grayness in the sky.

"I think it's Charleston."

"What time is it?"

I turn off the radio and it reverts to a clock.

"5:32."

"You mind dropping me somewhere?"

"Where?" I say.

"Anywhere."

"That old bit."

"I can't help it," she says. "I'm a free spirit."

"You're in a better mood."

"You didn't try anything."

"That's it?"

She looks out the window and again folds her arms, but she's lost the tightwire tension in her neck.

"You know that feeling?" she says. "As an adult you get it less and less because it's you who's responsible."

"What feeling?"

"Like when you go to sleep, and when you wake up, you're someplace else. You've rested and made progress all at the same time."

"This is a good thing?"

"It's good. Maybe it's one reason I like this."

She doesn't say what "this" is, not exactly, just keeps staring and points at a McDonald's after we turn down the off-ramp, and I let her out in the parking lot after handing her a twenty and telling her to eat breakfast.

"To start your day right," she says. "Healthy living."

And I nod and pull away, onto the highway, and then I'm driving through the mountains. The shapeless sun is in the sky, and the morning has no edges. I pull out the paper and write "Trese." And now I'm headed for a patch of morning fog that's rolling out of the trees and settling thick and blank and white across the lanes.

their own resolution

I was eleven and just out of band practice when my Dad appeared, his long tall body like a broken twig, leaning against his new truck in the parking lot of the middle school. He wore one of those yellow baseball caps with the plastic mesh in the back and a foam front that said, "*I need another set of beer goggles . . . she's still ugly.*"

I trudged up to him and set my tuba case on the ground.

"You're not going to wear that, are you?" I said.

"Barnabus, I already am."

My father, who I'd never seen drink a beer in his life, had in the past three weeks, as my sister put it, "gone off the rez."

"We're still going to see Mom tonight, right?"

He smiled. He was, I guess, what you'd call a handsome man, if somewhat on the overly lean side, unlike myself. I was 'large of bone' and undeniably unathletic. Pee-wee league football the year before had been disastrous; the helmet had fit so tight, it cut off blood to my brain and made my arm curl up involuntarily. I never went back. My consolation sport, the ping-pong club at the athletic center, had been equally a non-starter for numerous reasons.

"Did we say we were going to see Mom, tonight?" Dad jammed his fingers into the front pocket of his new Levi's, which were tighter than his old ones. There was a kind of ignoble and traumatizing bulge about the zipper, a scrotum-crushing denim bubble that reminded me of a water balloon being squeezed.

"Dad, it's important. And Mom'll flip if you don't."

He lifted my tuba into the back of the truck and secured it with a bungee cord. "How about we do something different, just you and me?"

Tonight's dinner, unequivocally, was to be the most important meal of my life. Plus, it went without saying most kids my age would rather die than hang out with their fathers. But Dad's new 'lifestyle,' as Mom called it, lent an edge of outrageous possibility to every undertaking.

"Like what?" I said.

He was thinking, touching his bare ring-finger with his thumb. I toyed with the idea of sending him a telepathic message—titty bar titty bar titty bar—a place I wasn't even sure how to picture, let alone if one existed in Ohio. A wild and lost kind of look had overtaken him lately, and he always held his gaze just over my head. It was going on four-thirty and the mid-autumn air felt charged with the dry early onset of dark. I kicked a few rocks.

"Watch the truck," he said. He stroked its pale side like a skittish perlino.

"You still thinking?" I said.

"You got suggestions?"

Titty bar, I mind-screamed.

"I suppose there's always chocolate sundaes," he said.

"Or beer." I pointed to his hat, and for a second he looked ashamed.

"You're too young for that."

"What about dinner with Mom? We could do that, like you told her you would."

"Or," he said, "what about target practice?"

There was no frame of reference. I'd never fired so much as a BB gun. So far as I knew, Dad hadn't either.

He opened the door to the truck and inside were two shotguns resting, butt ends on the floor, against the stickshift. White price tags still hung from the stock of each one. On the seat was a plastic Wal-Mart bag holding three boxes of shells.

I managed a croaky "What?" and Dad laughed. It wasn't a way I'd heard him laugh before.

"Check it out," he said. He pointed to the truck bed. I had to press right up against the wheel well to see the nine grocery bags bungeed next to my tuba case. Each bag contained two or three gallons of milk. Big white plastic jugs. If I'd thought of it then I might have found it funny: here was essentially what I would have seen at a titty bar.

"These," he said, "are for target practice. The cashier at the checkout line thought I was crazy."

• • •

The separation had been as swift as it was silent, the ninja of divorces. Mom and Dad never screamed at one another or held long family meetings in which my sister and I were made to hear the sordid details of their crumbling relationship. One day Dad left the house with a duffel bag of clothing. Mom cried in her room for two days before she sat me down in the living room. "You're going to go with your dad," she said, "We've decided both you and Joleen are at an age where you need to have someone in your life who can address your particular concerns."

Thankfully she never mentioned 'changing bodies,' but the rest of her speech had a legalistic ring to it.

"I'm doing it for you," she said. She dug her fingernails way down into the couch, then put her hands over my ears. She held my head. "A boy needs his dad," she said. I got the sense she'd rehearsed this part the most.

I didn't argue. Dad had been in a hotel while he sought out an apartment. When he came for me, he and mom treated each other like old friends in a supermarket. She mentioned my socks still in the washer and asked if we'd like to wait while they dried. He said no. We'd buy new ones.

My feet were rubbed raw with blisters for a week before he remembered.

•　•　•

We'd been driving in silence for nearly twenty minutes, the shotguns riding bitch between us, before I noticed the newly installed CB. It sat beneath the radio, mounted to the underside of the dash. Its coiled cord sprung and swayed with every bump.

"What's that?"

"Oh," he said, "are you addressing me?"

It had been three weeks since the official separation, and in that time I'd taken up a form of what I considered to be subtly malevolent protest. I couldn't avoid all communication, but there was plenty of time in transit together. My silence was aided by the racket of the truck. Dad called it the sound of the road. To me it sounded like pretension. He'd never been an especially outdoorsy or physical guy, and he'd never had use for a pickup. But its industrial tumult of bolts, the naked singing of its shocks, filled the space between us and hid my silence so I couldn't be accused of outright rebellion.

"What is it? A radio or something?"

"A citizens' band," he said. I could tell he'd been waiting for me to ask. "Forty channels. Want to listen?"

He turned the volume knob over with a click and the box came to life with a low static.

"We can talk to other truckers," he said.

"We're not truckers. We're in a truck, but we're not truckers."

"What should our code name be?" He picked up the mic, cupped it in his palm, and pressed down on the button. "Breaker breaker. This is the white hog comin' atcha, over."

21

The static returned. I held my breath.

"Breaker breaker," he said again. He fiddled with a knob labeled 'squelch.' The static changed tone, the sound like a handsaw being bent in a man's hands. "Breaker breaker, come back at me, good buddy."

We drove out of town, our ears bent toward the squawk box, our mouths open. He handed the mic over. "You try it."

"Can I give us a different name?"

"We can be whatever we want."

"Breaker breaker, this is. . . ." I was blanking. "White hawk," I said. "Anybody out there?"

We listened to static the whole way.

• • •

Tonight's dinner was a mandate. After being released into my father's custody, my new life with him was revoked almost as soon as it began. I'd been at school eating lunch when the vice principal marched me out of the cafeteria. I followed her into the hall still toting my corndog. She led me in silence directly into the principal's office where she sat me down alongside my mother.

My mother was a green-eyed woman who smelled strongly of Dove. She possessed farmer's hands, strong-fingered, a trait she claimed was her father's. A high pique had worked its way into her face, her skin flushed, her eyes watery. She looked like someone had doused her with a shot of pepper spray. Our principal, a heavyset man with a perpetually brown wardrobe, sat behind his desk. He didn't once look at me.

"I'm taking Barnabus home right now, and we're leaving the state," she told him.

"Mrs. Beiting, you know I can't allow that. Not until we contact your husband."

My parents had signed papers notifying the school of our new arrangement.

"Mr. Beiting is the primary caregiver, according to your own statement."

their own resolution

My mother pounded her farmer's fist into the arm of her chair. "Things have changed. I want him now."

The principal leaned back in his chair and crossed his thick fingers over his stomach. "I don't want to call the police."

"You call the police," she said. "You see what Sheriff Hamilton thinks of my husband—still legally married—what he thinks of his high school buddy, Dan Beiting, in the IGA supermarket holding hands with another man."

The principal looked my way.

I held up my half-eaten corndog. "His name is Ed," I offered.

•   •   •

I'd met Ed once, at a JV basketball game. I was first chair tuba in my fifth grade class, and I'd been selected as one of a dozen kids to come play 'Hang on Sloopy' with the high school band for half-time. I was sweaty and winded by the third quarter when the band director released us, and by the time I'd stowed my tuba in the trainer's room, Dad and this other man were in the hallway waiting for me.

"Great job, buddy," Dad said.

"You couldn't hear me."

"I could, too. You're the bassline, am I right? That song's nothing without a bassline. Am I right?"

He turned to the other man as if for confirmation. The man was slightly taller than my dad, more muscular and healthy-looking in a fitness-nut sort of way, but he looked older. He had a gray crew cut, which he rubbed somewhat nervously.

"I could hear it," the man said. "Sounded real good."

"This is my friend, Ed," Dad said. "I thought he'd like to hear you play. Ed was in the Ohio State Band. He played that song, 'Hang On, Sloopy.' Did you know it's the state rock song? He played it in the big time, so he knows what he's talking about."

Ed and I looked at one another.

"Could you really hear me?"

23

"Definitely," he said.

"I'm Barnabus." I held out my hand. Ed shook it, a single firm jolt.

"That's right," my Dad said. "I'm glad you guys met. I'm glad Ed got to hear you play."

•   •   •

Mom didn't take me from school. The principal talked her down like he'd been trained for such crises. Maybe he had. She called Dad that night and they set a date, the following Thursday, for dinner to reconsider the division of parental labor. What she meant was, she wanted me back. Dad was no longer suitable. I suppose she'd suspected, but the sighting in the grocery store had made it official.

Now it was Thursday—*the* Thursday—and Dad and I, instead of driving toward Mom's house, were dropping out of his truck holding shotguns and staring at a bald patch of land. Two massive oak stumps stood in the middle of a field of sallow clover. There were no houses for miles. I'd heard high school kids came out here to do it doggy-style on the stumps. Some of the kids called it hump-stump field, but it didn't look like anybody had been here in a long time. Maybe not ever.

"You ready?" Dad said.

"Are we still going to mom's?"

The tension in his neck and shoulders suddenly broke. He seemed to lose height. "Is that what you want? To go with your mom?"

"I don't know."

Dad and I had only been on our own a few weeks. Life was inscrutable. We were like an object tossed into the air, in that nanosecond, reaching our zenith before succumbing to gravity, a moment of perfect weightlessness when all forces seemed equal and all decisions impossible.

"I just don't know," I said.

"Why don't we do some shooting. Then we'll decide. We'll talk about it."

I pulled the price tag up around the barrel of the gun. It was a paper thing written by hand—$230—and it was tied with a thin piece of string. It came off with barely a snap. And like that, the gun felt like mine.

Evening was already shading the sky a murky eggplant color as we walked out to the middle of the field and Dad sat down on one of the stumps to quietly read the shotgun manual cover-to-cover.

"All right," he said. "I think we've got it. Just remember never to point the gun at anybody."

"Did the manual tell you that?"

"No need to be snarky. We're having fun here." He held up the sack of ammunition, then walked me through the function of the safety switch, the loading of shells, the sighting, the unsmooth action of the pump as it slid the shells into the chamber, a glimpse of red through the opening on the right side, and then we were ready to fire.

He set the first gallon of milk on the stump and we both walked back toward the truck, our guns pointed skyward. Dad rested the butt of his shotgun against his ribs so he carried it like a man in a movie. I held mine in a mock military way, crosswise in front of my chest. I imagined us looking like something we weren't, something more badass. Holding a gun gave me that feeling, like I was untouchable.

We walked almost all the way back to the truck and turned. We were about fifty yards from the stump. The milk jug looked miniscule and less dramatic from here.

"You ready?" he said.

I set my shotgun on the hood of the truck. Dad winked at me. Then he turned and fired.

The shot rang loud, and I clapped my hands to my ears. Dad opened his mouth like a man trying to yawn on a plane.

"Holy shit, that was loud," he said. It was the first time I'd heard him curse.

"Holy shit, that was loud," I repeated.

"Did I hit it?"

"You hit the grass," I said. "I saw dirt fly up."

He handed the gun off to me and went riffling through the glove box of the truck. I noticed he hadn't set the safety, so I did it myself. He came back with bits of tissue he'd twisted into little white tornado shapes.

"Stick these in your ears."

We looked like prop comedians making it appear as if handkerchiefs were going all the way through our brains. I tried smoothing my tissues down to give myself a more sleek look.

"Let's get closer," Dad said loudly. The volume of his voice made me doubt the effectiveness of the tissues.

With less ceremony, he stopped, looked down the barrel, and fired again. A chip of the stump on the right side splintered into the air.

"That was kind of cool," I said. The blast had been almost as ear-cracking as before.

"Must be something wrong with the sight," he said. He fired. No hit. He walked forward another ten yards. "Do you know what this dinner is going to be about?"

Fired again. Nothing but shredded clover.

"I know it's about you and Ed," I shouted.

"Lets get closer." Another fifteen yards, and he shot again. This time the milk jug moved just a little. An anemic spurt of white dribbled out the right side of it and onto the stump, making a sickly little pool that ran down the bark.

Dad took another few steps. His face changed suddenly. He was no longer looking at me. I could hear he was cursing under his breath in a long string. He walked right up on the stump, his face twisted, jaw clenched, and pulled back on the trigger. The gun didn't go off.

"Shit," he said loudly. "Shit!"

He turned to me, holding his gun toward the ground, like all the shooting had worn him out. "Do you understand any of this, Barnabus?"

"You went gay," I said.

His mouth bloomed into a weak smile. He laughed in that new way he had of laughing. He looked down at the

26

gun. For a moment it felt like we might fall into one of those quiet reveries. But he rallied. "You going to fire one of these or what?"

I was waiting for something else, for more words, but he just made a shooing gesture. I ran back toward the truck.

"Walk it back," he shouted.

I brought my loaded gun to the stump so I was only ten feet away, and Dad said, "Whenever you're ready."

I held up the shotgun. It was heavy. My arms shook. In the end a gun is just a cluster of metal pieces being held against the soft flesh of a human being. It felt exactly that way, unnatural, as I pointed it at the jug, which had leaked about halfway down. I could make out the shredded hole in the jug's side where Dad had winged it.

"Before I married your mother," Dad said, "I thought I might be different."

I lowered the gun. I wanted my own new milk jug to shoot. Aiming at the half-emptied one felt like I was being cheated. I wanted to cause a whole and unbroken thing to explode.

"Some men from church," Dad said, "good friends of ours, came and talked to me. We took a walk in the woods, and they brought a Bible with them. I want you to know this, okay?"

I looked around for the other milk gallons, but they were all back in the truck.

"We prayed a lot about it. They were trying to help, is what I'm saying. They thought the way I am—the way I am now—they thought it was a sin. You're mom thinks I'm trying to hurt her. I'm not."

"It's okay, Dad," I said.

I only said this to make him stop talking, because it gave me a weak and nauseous feeling to see him like that, with the ridiculous tissues coming out of his ears and the vulgar yellow hat and him still holding the gun and looking at the stump. I wished I were somewhere else. The thrill had dissipated, and the gun was too heavy. My Dad kept talking because there was no one else but me.

"You're seeing me at my worst, Barnabus." He took off the hat and set it over the milk jug so it almost covered the empty portion. With the hat over top of it, the jug's fat white bottom looked full and tempting again.

I lifted the gun. Dad stepped back as I walked up to the jug point blank. And fired.

The hat and the jug exploded. The rifle recoiled. I'd been holding the butt against my chest instead of my shoulder, and it was like a full grown man punched me in the heart. I dropped the gun and fell backward in the grass. I opened my mouth, but my lungs wouldn't work. No in. No out.

My father placed a hand on me, sat me up.

"You just got the wind knocked out of you, that's all," he said. "You'll be all right. You just lost your wind."

Tears. Panic. I couldn't breathe. I looked around for help, but there was only my dad.

Then slowly, slowly, slowly, the air came. I could see the relief on his face.

"Barnabus," he said, "I've decided to bring Ed to dinner tonight."

• • •

We drove in our customary silence, the hair on my dad's hatless head looking greasy and smashed. A grim stillness had overtaken his eyes. Twenty-three milk jugs jiggled in the back of the truck, untouched. After the shot that did away with the hat and left a deep and purpling bruise over my heart, we hadn't even talked about setting up more.

Dad reached out and put a hand on my shoulder. He didn't take his eyes off the road.

"Barnabus, I want you to tell me what you want. Before we go in there, I want to know who you want to live with."

I'd fallen back into my old despondency. My Dad was a failure, I thought, a failure at living. The most hurtful thing I could do was remain silent. I did that.

We made the left into town just as he let out a childish

whimper. Even in the dark I could see his face. It had gone red with strain and his mouth had curved down.

"Barnabus," he whispered. "I'm trying."

I didn't answer. I'd never hated him more. I wanted him to suffer, and the more he cried, the more I felt my silence solidifying into a blunt and heavy weapon.

"Okay," he said. "Okay."

•   •   •

When I was very young, from age two to about five, I would always get croup in the winters. I'd lie down at night and within an hour I'd wake up struggling to breathe, the feeling of sand in the back of my throat touched off by a terrifying constriction in my chest. I'd cough and cough and cough, the sound low and loud, barking. It was the sound, I imagined, of a bear cub struggling against a chain pulled tight around its neck. It was the sound of something dying just a little.

When I woke up those nights with croup, hacking, nothing coming up but the restless dead-air as I gripped the sheets into two twisted bunches between my fingers, I would hear my dad's footsteps in the hallway, his stumbling, heavy footfall coming to the open door and crossing to my bed. I would feel his hand on my forehead, then his fingers beneath my armpits as he lifted me up, held me against him, my body still tense with the exertion of breathing as he carried me down to the basement. Attached to the basement was our garage, which had been built into the side of a hill. The December wind I could hear and feel through the garage door. Dad would set me down and tell me, "Breathe, buddy. Breathe." His hand on my back, rubbing, he would repeat this over and over until the cold air flowed down my throat and turned whatever sand there was into an icy, eased breath, a still tremulous but now settled intake that filled the inside of me with a numb and quiet peace. I grew sleepy again on my feet as he kept rubbing and rubbing that hand against my back.

going anywhere

"Breathe, buddy. Breathe," he whispered. And I did.

• • •

Ed met us at our house—Mom and Joleen's house. He stood in the dark across the street with his arms crossed over his broad chest. A pair of wide and unfashionable glasses made his crew cut look all the more unstylish.

"Barnabus," he said as Dad and I got out of the truck. He held out a hand to shake, but I pretended not to see. I headed toward the house without looking back.

Ed must have seen that my Dad had been crying.

"You okay, Dan?"

"Forget it."

We crossed the lawn and Joleen was already opening the door and staring across the broad, gray-painted, wooden porch with its swing and the wicker furniture that all seemed inviting in an already foreign and lost way to me.

"Mom says you guys are late," she said. Joleen had very dark hair, like my dad's. The bangs on her forehead had a doll-like neatness to them, lending her smirk an artificial look. Then she caught sight of Ed. Her face lost its judgmental woodenness and, sapped of color, slackened into something like a village idiot.

"Is that—"

"What's for dinner?" I said.

She pulled the door back and allowed us to enter. We stood in the foyer of what had been our own house only a month ago, now made the strangest place on earth for its intimate inhospitality.

Joleen slid away behind us and disappeared down the hallway. I could hear her hissing, "Mom mom mom."

To the right was our sturdy dining room set. Through the doorway at the back was the kitchen. A few minutes passed before Mom emerged from it carrying a casserole pan. Joleen was close behind. Mom had plastered a disturbing grin across her face and held out the dish rigidly, like a human forklift, lowering it onto the middle of the table.

In the three weeks I'd been living with Dad alone in the new apartment off Swenson, I hadn't once had a home-cooked meal. There were nights Dad picked up food from the Arby's down the street, or we settled into a booth at the Toro Loco when he felt like splurging. But most nights it was catch-as-catch-can—PB and J, microwaved hot dogs, tuna with tennis-ball-sized blobs of mayo. So the smell of what I thought might be Mom's famous oyster stuffing was enough to send a shiver through my gut.

She looked at me pointedly. "I've cooked rolls, too. And baked mac and cheese. And chicken soup and carved turkey."

"It's like Thanksgiving," Joleen added.

Mom made a sweeping gesture toward the chairs—"Sit. Everyone, sit."—then fled back to the kitchen.

• • •

Halfway through the meal Mom still hadn't made eye contact with Dad or Ed. Neither of them had said a word. Joleen and I tried a little school conversation, but it fizzled when I failed to understand what she meant by the "x-axis and y-axis," which was apparently integral to getting a joke her geometry teacher told during fifth period.

With the silence slowly filling the room, the food became increasingly bitter in my mouth. A lump of congealed mac and cheese wobbled on my plate as I poked it with a fork. The room felt suddenly hot, then irreversibly cold, then hot again.

I had to make something happen. I had to get everybody talking. I looked at Mom and said, "Dad took me out to hump-stump field."

I hadn't meant to phrase it that way. But the field's reputation must have extended across generation lines. Mom addressed Dad directly: "You took him out there?"

Dad nodded.

Mom stood. She held either side of her plate like she was actively trying to resist winging it Frisbee-style at my father's head.

31

"You goddamn son of a bitch," she said.

As for mom, I had only heard her curse one other time. Until a few weeks ago we'd been a pretty strait-laced family. No cursing. No Lord's name in vain.

Her jaw worked itself into a tight and grinding thing. Her mouth withered into a slit. "You son of a bitch. You don't think it's enough you expose our children to this scandal, you make him sit in the car while you—" She turned on me. "Did you see anything? Was he there?" She pointed at Ed. "Is that where they met up?"

Without waiting for me to answer, she held up her plate of food with both hands and snapped it in two across her knee. Food went flying to either side of her. Ed stood up. Dad made a choking noise. Joleen had turned into a statue.

"Marisa," Dad said, "calm down."

Mom dropped her plate-halves and reached for the nearest dish, the tureen of chicken soup. She knocked aside the lid and stuck her hand in, pulled out a wad of homemade noodles and chucked them at Dad. They scattered mid-air in a wide arc, finding the walls, the table, Dad's shirt. One noodle struck the window and stayed there, fascinatingly unmoved by gravity.

"Marisa, calm down," my Dad said more forcefully.

Ed rubbed his gray hair front to back.

"Mom," I said. "It wasn't like that. I shot a gun."

I couldn't have picked a worse addendum.

She stared at me. Her gray-green eyes had never been so wide. "Barnabus, go to your room."

I opened my mouth and nothing came out. I rose and retreated to the foyer. Joleen followed. And I suddenly realized I didn't belong here. Mom had kept my room pretty much intact, but it didn't have my broken-spined *Lord of the Rings* set with the torn cardboard box. My sweaters were all gone. My dresser and underwear, the wedges I'd used in a science fair project on simple machines, my school notebooks, a poem written on red construction paper about Civil War soldiers which won me third place in the arts fair, even my games—they'd all been transported, given new and designated homes in certain corners of my new closet, my new room. All I could think of was that upstairs, in my old room, were the old socks I never got back. I didn't want them.

"I'm leaving," I said.

I left through the front door and Joleen trailed me.

"Do you want to see a shotgun?" I said. "It's in the truck."

"Should we call the police?"

I didn't know if Mom would calm down or kill Dad and Ed, but I said, "It'll be all right."

I walked Joleen across the street and opened the truck. Dad had left it unlocked. The guns were still there. I could see the little red button of the safety, still up, where Dad had failed to set it again. Joleen was looking shaky. I walked her around to the passenger side, away from the road, and made her sit down in the footwell with her feet hanging down into the grass.

"Why do you think Dad is acting this way?" she said.

"I don't know." I still didn't want to think about it. I wanted to show Joleen how to load a gun. I found the shells and demonstrated by replacing the one I'd fired. I made sure Joleen saw, but I didn't explain it. I just pumped the gun until I heard it click. Untouchable, I thought, and got that same sense of being a badass. Joleen looked silently impressed.

"Do you know how to use that?"

I sighted the branch of a nearby tree as if I were checking some vital specifications. "I think Dad and Ed have known each other a long time."

"He looks like a gym teacher."

"I think maybe he and Dad love each other." I thought about the way Ed asked Dad if he were okay. It bothered me the way he'd said my dad's name: You okay, Dan?

"Ugh," Joleen said. "Gross. It's so stupid."

"Mom's been kind of mean to Dad."

"She's always a little mean. She's tough."

"Maybe Dad didn't want tough," I said.

"Still," Joleen said.

"Still."

"Have you ever heard mom cuss?"

"I heard both of them cuss today. I think they must be angry. I think that's it."

"Gee, you think, dummy?"

"Yeah, I think. And yes, I heard mom cuss once."

"When?"

Mom had laughed when she said it. We'd been in the attic looking for a humidifier my Dad swore was up there and I'd found a crate of records, all sitting up straight and filed in alphabetical order. I'd pulled the first one out. It was an ABBA album. Mom said the records were from when she was a girl. She said it was a shame we didn't have a record player anymore. She flipped through them and pulled out one that was a recording of the Ohio State band.

"I used to listen to this all the time when I was about your age," she said. "I wanted to be in that band."

"Were you?"

"No. I played the flute in high school, but I went to a community college. They didn't have a band."

She read the songs listed on the back of the album. "Best damn band in the land."

I must have gasped at that word "damn," because she held out a hand to me. "Sorry, no. You know we're not supposed to curse. That's what they called the OSU band. Best d*** band in the land. They called them that."

"Oh," I said. And Mom had laughed. She'd laughed maybe because she and Dad had taught us a certain way. Maybe even then, in the back of her mind, she found it silly. Maybe now, too, and that's why she spoke the way she did over the dinner table, because it was such a small thing, the language, compared to what was happening.

I told Joleen, "Mom said 'damn' once."

"Big deal," she said.

I carried the gun around to the back of the truck and

Joleen followed me. Behind us was parked a white Hyundai with one of those Ohio State license-plate frames. There was the block O with a little buckeye leaf inside.

"Ed was in the Ohio State band," I said.

"So?"

"So, this is his car."

I pointed the barrel at his license plate and pretended to sight the gun again. Really I was just reading the letters on the plate over and over again. PDR-6547. It wasn't even a vanity plate or anything. It was just random.

"I don't think Dad really wants me to live with him any-more. He says he does, but I think he's just scared."

"He called me on the phone and told me he was sorry."

"He tells me that all the time now."

I left the gun trained on the license plate. I wondered what it would be like to blow up a car. I wanted Dad to quit telling me things. I wanted him to be quiet and quit crying. I wanted Mom to be someone else.

"I'm going to shoot out his windshield," I said.

Joleen stayed quiet.

I didn't fire. I put the gun down in the grass and waved for Joleen to help me. I climbed into the back of the truck. From the bed of it I could see the open sunroof of Ed's car. I handed the jugs down to Joleen, and we worked silently, without words, as sisters and brothers can some-times do. She stood on the hood of the car, and I broke the seals on the milk caps. I handed them up to her and she poured them through the sunroof. She moved left to right, and when she got tired, I traded her places, mak-ing certain the milk splashed down over the console, the emergency brake, puddled in the seats, sloshed over the seatbelts. I lowered my arm in and slung one jug clear into the back window. It made a loud, plastic *boonk* which finished with a satisfying dislodging of all of its liquids into the speakers.

We finished with all twenty-three gallons and still no one had come out of the house.

"Do you think we'll have to go live with someone else?" Joleen said.

"Why would we have to do that?"

"What if Mom can't afford to take care of us?"

Mom worked as a secretary in an insurance office. I had no idea what that paid. I hadn't thought of the same things Joleen thought about. I'd only thought about how I hated Dad and how I hated Mom, and Ed, too, and how I just wanted to be left alone.

"Barnabus," Joleen said. She nodded toward the house. Ed emerged. His hands were in his pockets, his head down.

I ran the shotgun back to the truck. I started kicking empty milk jugs away from the car. Joleen did the same.

Ed approached us as if he didn't notice. He said, "Hi."

We nodded.

Ed leaned against the front of his car. I was positive he would hear the milk sloshing around inside. He ran his hand back over his crew cut and adjusted his glasses. Joleen and I waited, our hands behind our backs.

Finally, he said, "Did you know 'Hang on Sloopy' is the state rock song?"

I stared him down.

"'Hang on Sloopy.' That song you played at the basketball game last year?"

"I know what it is," I said.

"Okay," he said. "Did you know it's Ohio's state rock song? Not every state has one. It's by a band called the McCoys. Kind of a one-hit wonder group. They were from Ohio."

"I don't care," I said.

Joleen's eyes kept wandering to the interior of the car.

"I just thought you might find it interesting," he said. "It was about an old jazz singer. That was Sloopy. They made us remember a bunch of these facts when we were in the OSU band. You had to recite them your first year as part of your hazing."

"What's hazing?" Joleen said.

"Just some stuff they made us go through to be part of

36

the band. Like for instance we had to recite the resolution that, you know, ratified it as the state song. I still remember parts of it."

He stood up and looked forward as if standing at attention, then gave a curt salute and began speaking in a military sort of voice. "Whereas, in 1965, an Ohio-based rock group known as the McCoys blah blah blah and then an arranger for the Ohio State University Marching Band created the band's now famous arrangement of 'Sloopy,' first performed at the Ohio State-Illinois football game on October 9, 1965; and whereas if fans of jazz, country-western, classical, Hawaiian, and polka music think those styles should be recognized, then by golly, they can push their own resolution; and whereas 'Hang on Sloopy' is of particular relevance to the baby boom generation, who were once dismissed as a bunch of long-haired, crazy kids, but who are now old enough to vote in sufficient numbers to be taken seriously, and whereas adoption of this resolution will not take too long, cost the state anything, or affect the quality of life in this state to any appreciable degree, and if we in the legislature just go ahead and pass the darn thing, we can get on with more important stuff."

He relaxed as if being commanded to do so and said in his normal voice, "Isn't that wild? They actually wrote all that in the resolution. I still remember most of it. Can't remember the Shakespeare sonnets from senior English. I can't remember any part of *The Sound of Music*, not even the songs—and I was Captain Georg. But I remember most of that resolution."

I pulled my shoulders up around my ears in a theatrical shrug to show him how much I thought of all that, but he seemed unfazed.

"You get that CB to work?" he said.

He knew about the CB. Right then I understood Dad and Ed had been talking this whole time. They were partners. I hadn't seen it. Mom hadn't either. Joleen certainly hadn't seen it. But everything Dad had become in the past few weeks, some searching for identity, had spilled forth in a ridiculous mess of mixed messages and failed attempts from years of an underground river backing up slowly slowly slowly.

"The CB doesn't work," I said. It was more to shut him up than start a conversation. He seemed to take this as a challenge. He walked to the truck and opened the passenger door. He made a face at the guns, then clicked the safety on Dad's and set them aside. He turned on the CB and ran the gamut of dials until he found a number that suited him. Then he fiddled a bit more with the squelch until the static made a low, even hum.

He spoke into the mic. "This is Little-Bo-Beep-Lost-Sheep, you hear me out there?" He released the mic and whispered to me, "Dukes of Hazard reference. You ever see it?"

I shook my head. I wanted to walk away, but, like my dad, he'd hooked me. I couldn't help but wait for an answer.

It came.

"This is the Schlitz Bitch, 10-2 Bo-Beep, how's the road?"

I couldn't believe it. Some surly-eyed trucker traveling the snaking, dark roads, his seat springs sighing in the quiet of his cab, his neck itching and razor-burned beneath his beard, his stomach yearning for a country-fried steak at the next stop—that man, that voice in the hollow and empty night, was out there. Or maybe he was anybody. Someone else, someone I couldn't imagine, but the long and short of it was he was out there and he'd heard us.

Ed pressed the mic again. "10-4, Bubba Schlitz. You rolling on 32?"

"That's a ten."

"Hey, uh, if you're headed west past Pickering, watch out for heavy gators and destruction up the county line. Looks like maybe a 10-42 pretty recent." Again he released the button and addressed me. "That's a construction sight, and some tire bits. You ever see those on the highway?"

Again he spoke into the mic. "Probably means you'll have a few bears, Schlitzy. Watch yourself, keep the shiny side up, brother."

"Preciate it, Bo-Beep. Same to ya."

And that was it.

"What did you say?" I asked.

"I said there might have been an accident and some cops. I don't know if any of it's true, but it's not going to hurt him to stay a little alert and slow down some." He mimicked my exaggerated shrug. "And that's that."

"Can you teach me?"

"I can," he said. "Just don't ever say, 'good buddy,' like they do in the movies."

"Why?"

"Just don't. It means 'queer.'"

"Like you?" Joleen said. She was standing behind me, her eyes little black slits. "You made Mom and Dad break up."

And now a strange thing happened.

I felt defensive of Ed. I turned on Joleen. "You don't know anything," I said. "Dad was a queer a long time ago and they tried to stop him with the Bible."

Joleen took a step backward. She pointed at Ed. "He's faking," she said. "He's being something he's not. He's not a trucker."

"You don't know anything," I said.

Ed came between us and put out a hand. "I don't want this to be a fight," he said. "I just want—I can't help this—"

He turned around abruptly and walked to his car.

All I was thinking was that I wished Ed were my dad. I wished I were going with him.

He unlocked his door and sat, pulling the door shut. It was only an instant, a half-second, but I saw it, that flash of shock as he sat in that wet, cold seat. I wanted to cry. I wanted to take it all back, because Ed, I was certain, was my real father, the man I was meant to have. He knew about the tuba and about the CB, and he probably knew about guns. He was all the things my Dad wanted to be but had missed out on because he had a family, and there was only that, only me and Joleen and Mom.

Ed held the handle of his door as if he were about to open it again. I balled my fists. Then I saw his shoulders fall. It was like Dad out in the field when he'd seemed so tired. Ed looked broken. I took a short step toward the car. I wanted to apologize, to take it back.

Then something inexplicable happened. Ed lifted his face and grinned. He gave us a polite wave and started the car. For a moment I wondered if he'd noticed. Maybe I'd misinterpreted his earlier shock. He slowly pulled away from the curb, his smile wider than before. He was waving like a man who doesn't have twenty-three gallons of milk making little tidal pools around his ankles.

Then Dad was coming out of the house, his hands jammed into his tight jeans looking like a man hunched against a storm. Mom was behind him at the open door, but she wasn't screaming. She was lowering herself to her knees in the doorway and she was beckoning to Joleen and me with both hands. I could see she'd been crying now too, and it melted the hardness of her face, the rigid lines losing definition in the soft glow trailing out of the windows of the house. The porchlight wasn't on, and she was more of a mellow silhouette, scooping at the air, gesturing for us both to come, and I knew what had been decided by the way she used both arms. Joleen and I passed Dad on the sidewalk, and he held out one hand and touched my shoulder as he passed me. And Mom was saying it's going to be okay, it's going to be, everything, all okay.

And I was holding her then, my mom, and Joleen, and we were down to a little family of three, and the night was coming up, and Dad's truck was snarling to life, and then it was gone until all I could think of was the fact that I hadn't seen his face. Right then it felt like I'd missed something so important as to warrant a gap, a fissure severing the reality of things for that one moment, because I'd missed it. I hadn't paid enough attention, and I'd lost my dad's face for good.

All I was left with was the sight of Ed as he drove away from the curb. I could picture that better than my father and it's what I think of now when I hear that song sometimes on the radio or at football games.

Hang on Sloopy, it says. Sloopy, it says, lives in a very bad part of town, and everybody, yeah, tries to put my Sloopy down. Well, Sloopy, I don't care what your daddy do. 'Cause you know, Sloopy girl, I'm in love with you.

That's what the song says.

And so I say now, Hang on Sloopy, hang on. Hang on Sloopy, hang on.

I think of Ed pulling away from us, smiling, as if nothing in the world could ever touch him.

hear it

He has the blunt, hard knuckles of a streetfighter. Hairy in multiple ways, he wears a brown serviceman's shirt with the name Cal embroidered across a patch on the left breast. He raises his fist at me.

"I'm gonna knock your teeth in, bud."

Summer heat like hellfire swoons across the oil-soaked concrete of the service station, and relentless blasts of it roll over us in waves as we stand in front of the little clerk's counter. It's a backroad, backcountry, and *Plummer's Sup and Pump* crouches in the shade of a fleshy green hill. I haven't had water for hours. My mouth tastes like that grime-caked nickel Jason Crabtree found on the floor of the bus and dared me to lick when we were in fifth grade. Twenty years ago? Why can't I remember how old I am?

"I don't have any problem with you," I say. Cal's shirt is unbuttoned and it's nothing but paunch and black hair and a scar running pink over his heart that looks like a knife slash. He's sweating, and his nose is shovel-pummeled flat.

"You the one started it," he says. He looks at the clerk,

some high school kid with a lazy eye, who holds up his hands like he's being robbed and takes a step back. Then Cal looks at the dog. It's gray and wire-haired and medium-sized, and it's wandered in from somewhere. It's sitting by a shelf of Hostess cakes near the two-liters of Mountain Dew, and there's a patch of fur on its left hip matted by either blood or oil or mange.

Cal says to me, "You think you're better than me, I'll fucking whoop your ass."

There's no one else around. We're in some rural tangle of wooded hills, the establishment set back off a slim S-curve county road in southern Ohio, some verdant dark dense place, and it's just me and Cal and the dog and the kid.

"Seriously," I say. "I didn't mean to offend you."

"You know what," Cal says. "I'm fucking tired of fucking people like you backing out when they find out I ain't stupid. 'Sorry' don't fucking cut it. Now, you gonna step outside or I'm going to go get my tire iron."

"I don't think you're stupid."

"You just tried to tell me that goddamn dog talked."

"Did I say that?"

"Don't fucking play dumb. Two minutes ago you said that goddamn dog talked like I'd believe it, like some kind of fucking asshole idiot."

"I didn't."

Or I did.

Low on gas. No water. Summer heat. I've been driving for hours. I walked in, and the dog spoke. I'm too hot and the dog spoke. I told Cal, I looked over and told him just that. I asked if he heard what the dog said. He took offense.

"Trying to play some fucking joke on me?" Cal says. "I'll fucking bust ya."

"I didn't," I say.

But I did.

The dog said the word 'spaghetti.'

The dog said it just as I walked in. I wanted someone to

confirm what I heard, so I turned to the man by the rack of direct-to-video DVDs, $3.99, the bargain bin of brown jersey gloves like a barrel of dead birds, that little display of Rol-Aids, Wintergreen flavor. Cal was standing there trying on a pair of cheap sunglasses, and I said to him, 'Did you hear that dog? That dog just talked. It said spaghetti.'

That's what I said to Cal.

"I wasn't trying to trick you," I say. "I really did. I heard it talk."

I look at the dog and hope it'll give me some kind of sign, some wink or translatable nod to let me know the words are coming again, that they're about to fall from its jowls.

The dog pants and nibbles at its paw.

It's funny though. It is funny. That the dog said 'spaghetti,' I realize. It's funny since Christy dropped the hot water, the whole pot of pasta on her foot—was that today? Yes. Today, at lunch. We were fighting and she turned and caught the bottom of the pan on the edge of the sink. The force of it wrenched the pot out of her fingers, and she dropped it and the water burned her foot, and I was yanking her sock off, and that's when she told me she'd had an affair.

She said, "I couldn't get over it. I wanted one, too," like it was a comfortable jacket or a new car. She wanted one, like me. She wanted that 'new affair' smell. So it's funny the dog, of all the words to say, should say spaghetti.

"You son of a bitch," Cal says. He pokes his index finger, grimy and solid, into my chest. "Get your fucking ass out there."

He shoves again.

It's funny the dog should say spaghetti because he could have said anything. Maybe 'Sophie,' the woman in the cubicle across from mine. Might have said 'mistake' or 'Belinda,' Christy's mom, where she went to stay for a month. Or 'radiator' because the car I drive is most definitely *not* new, not at all, and it overheats in the hills, when the temperature pushes ninety, and I have to run the heater, have the windows open, to keep it from breaking down. It gets hot,

44

maybe too hot, but it's better than being stranded. The dog might have said 'hot' even.

"Don't fucking roll your eyes at me," Cal says. "You ain't stalling, and I ain't waiting."

Both hands, he gives me a righteous push, and all the injustices of his life are behind it. I can feel them. He's fighting back. Because at some point you find out you've been wronged.

"Wait," I say. I point to the dog. "Maybe if we get closer. You'll hear it."

"Bud, if you think for one goddamn second—"

I drop to all fours and crawl over to the dog. I'm still so thirsty, and there's something on my head like a knit cap, and it feels tight. I keep feeling my head, the top of it, my hair, and there's nothing there. And I wonder if the dog might say 'hat' or tell me something that makes sense.

It really is funny he should have said 'spaghetti.' If a dog were going to say anything, you'd expect it to be one syllable, two at the most.

"Hey, boy," I say. "Hey."

"It's a girl," the clerk says. He's still standing back from the counter. He hasn't made any move to call the authorities. It may not have occurred to him.

"Hey, girl," I say.

"Her name's Sheila," the clerk says. He apparently wants to hear the dog speak as much as I do.

"Sheila," I say, sort of whispering. "Sheeeeeila. Spaghetti. Can you say 'spaghetti'?"

"You coward piece of shit," Cal says, and pulls me up to my feet. I'm looking at his chest and his ugly face, the black scruff on his jaws, the receding hairline, scratched-up leather belt, and the work boots all dark from wear. I wonder if Cal and I might have been friends. Maybe if we were neighbors we'd have shared beers on summer nights like the one only a few hours away. Maybe I'd lend him something like our shop-vac, and he'd return it, the motor burnt up and the hose all greasy, and he'd call it a piece of shit, and not offer to pay for it. Or maybe Christy and I would look after his two kids when he went in for that open-heart surgery, and he'd keep thanking us by bringing over his mom's oyster casserole, because she was grateful to have sat with her son in recovery, not having to worry about her grandbabies.

If the dog knows 'spaghetti,' maybe she knows something else. Something about Cal that throws this whole mix-up into perspective.

I drop back down. I'm leaned way over in the dog's face, and its breath is like that hot wind with a little rot baked in from some dead animal she's probably scavenged in a ditch just this morning.

And now I'm wondering if Sheila has a dog-husband somewhere and if she's ever cheated on him. Sweat is sliding up my spine. It's going in mad rivulets around my ribs and dripping into the front of my shirt. It's on my chin and on my lips, and that hat-feeling, that constricted feeling of a halo jammed down around my skull, that feeling is back. And the sweat is on my thighs under my pants, and I'm wondering why I didn't wear shorts to take this drive. I'm wondering where Christy got the gall to come back and say we'd work on it and then—after all that; that month away and the weeping in the bedroom over the phone, the both of us—after all that, she'd go and sleep with that absolute asshole, Shane Mercer, that—literally, I'm talking literally now—used car salesman. And that's what I've been thinking this afternoon, just driving, anywhere, driving, until I didn't notice that invisible fire flowing up off the asphalt and boiling the air, or the gas getting lower and lower, is that that's pretty damn tawdry, pretty cliché, a used car salesman in a small town after all the nights crying.

She said she was going to fix us lunch, a nice lunch, spaghetti with a good sauce she pulled off the internet, a garlic bread and a dessert she bought special, and she was going to tell me about Shane and we were going to push past it, but then the water spilled, and the spaghetti was all around her foot in the boiling water and she was kicking it and the noodles were everywhere. Absolutely everywhere, and it was all so hot, and I called the ambulance and left.

Shane fucking Mercer. I could have beat him to death on the hood of some used Volvo, $8,999 with money down.

"Come on, Sheila," I say to the dog. "Just a word. You want to say something about Cal?"

Cal gives me a boot to the ribs. "Get the fuck up."

The dog whines. There's a combination of syllables in there, a scrunched-up succession of consonants.

"What?" I say.

"I said get the fuck up."

"Not you."

The dog yawns, but right there at the end, there's that high-pitched sound dogs make at the tail-finish of a yawn. Was it 'hairy'? Haaaeeeriiaa. More like that. That high sound.

Cal hauls me up again, shoves me toward the open door. We're outside now in the baking light, the dense air, the curdled smell of life rolling down out of the wooded hills, fusing with the dumpster-sweetness, the diesel and garbage perfume.

Cal takes off that shirt. His muscled shoulders are two broad lumps on either side of his ugly head.

"The dog said something," I say.

"Bullshit."

That scar across his heart is blurring pink and angry in the sun, slick through the dark hair of his chest. Hairy, the dog said. Or maybe something else. Cal shakes out his arms and re-tightens his fists.

"Cal, I don't want to fight, okay? Okay, Cal?"

"My fucking name isn't Cal."

"It says Cal," I say. I point to his shirt on the ground in the oil.

"You throwing that in my face now? You saying Goodwill ain't good enough? You saying I can't buy a goddamn second-hand shirt?"

He belts me, right-handed, across my left cheek. The inside of his fist connects, and I'm lucky, I'm lucky he didn't catch me with the hammer-end, that cracked and solid row of knuckles. I wobble and think about making a run for the car, but it's no good.

"My goddamn name is Larry," he says.

Larry. The dog was saying Larry. If I could have listened harder, I would have heard it. No, the man who used to be Cal draws his arm back slowly, and shoots it forward into my stomach.

It's the heat and smells now, and the sounds are all gone. If I'd heard just a little better, but the blood is pounding in my ears. Larry's whooping me, like he said. He's whooping me, pushing back, at me and at his tired, poor, angry, dirty life, and I didn't hear. If I had, I wouldn't be staring, stupid, mute and soundless as the world disappears. My vision wouldn't be fading down to nothing, just a round telescope-vision of what's in front of me. I would have heard Christy breathing at the table before either of our transgressions—I'd have heard the way she tapped the chair kind of nervous, even after all these years of being married, and I'd have heard in her tapping she cared and we were still tucked away in it, in the love thing, after all the time together still holding on to one another because it was the best thing going. With her hands tapping the chair—not this hard blunt smack and thump—that nervous tap about something, about whatever, it didn't matter, and we were together, and then that week I went and slept with someone else. If I'd have heard what she was saying between the tapping, maybe about buying two-percent milk or some shooting in a public park, or something she'd been thinking about and was trying to share, I wouldn't be here, just staring, not hearing and now just seeing, just looking forward, gazing into the pink scar over another man's heart.

courier

From a certain angle he could make out her naked back, the chair where she was seated, the table and her elbow resting there. Most thrilling though was the triangle of space between arm and shoulder blade, that soft underside of her breast, fleshly, curved, and rosy-pale as a dream. Every morning.

Hormonal instinct had permanently changed his circadian cycle, making the alarm clock moot. Just before six Eliman sat up, slid off the bed, and puttered down the hall to the bathroom. Back in thirty seconds without waking another soul, he gently pulled the pitted chair from beneath his desk and sat. His old Star Wars sheets hung from the brass curtain rod over his window, and he held them back very slightly, the cotton cool in his hand because it was late in the year and his mother still left his room open to the night air. She told him it would keep his lungs clear.

He'd never been anywhere, seen anything. They had lived in Charityburg Eliman's entire life. A bedroom community for millworkers, the town never went through an identity crisis. For ninety years the oaks had grown fat, the sidewalks shady. Storefronts glistered in the spring rains and glowed forth with the candy-cane colors of holiday displays in winter. When the mills shut down, the workers began longer commutes to Columbus and destinations north, but kept Charityburg to themselves. The nearest Wal-Mart was fifteen miles away in Harris.

Eliman didn't think about this—the town and its history, or the lives of the people in it. Thirty feet from his window sat a house very like their own, with the single-car garage and an attic, a cool basement with cracks in the cinderblock wall, and this one anomaly, a naked woman in the kitchen, at the day's most delicate hour, sipping her coffee.

Her reasons? Eliman couldn't fathom. Being homeschooled, he often suspected he was being left out of something, some information to which sixth graders (his age) or tenth graders (at whose aptitude levels he wrote and did math) were privy. Perhaps he'd missed some common, schoolyard knowledge about women—pearl-skinned ladies about his mother's age; these dark-haired beauties in their homes without husbands or children.

"I see you," he whispered into the half-light.

As with every morning, the woman stood up and slid out of sight without a glimpse of any more parts, no matter how Eliman leaned. He yanked a spiral-bound notebook from beneath his mattress. The rings made a zipping sound as they pulled free. By now several pages had been filled. He turned to the first blank line and recorded. November fifth, the letter 'N,' beside it the word "coffee." In the beginning, there'd sometimes been the letter 'R'. Also notations like "oatmeal" and "toast" and "smoothie." But lately only coffee; only 'N.'

If his mother ever found the notebook, he'd tell her he was keeping a record of what the mailman, James, had eaten for breakfast. He'd tell her he'd been observing James as part of a social experiment—'N' for 'Nice,' 'R' for 'Reserved' to denote how James acted that day. He'd tell her he was looking for a correlation between mood and diet.

In reality, the 'R' stood for robe. The 'N' for naked. And it had nothing to do with James.

• • •

He read all morning and at noon set aside *The Silmarillion* to march into his own Thangorodrim. He imagined the volcanoes of Morgoth rising before him, some igneous thrust of razor-edged rock rising out of the laundry room. The kitchen, like Angband, the dark fortress in the Iron Mountains, had in the past month grown full of dangers. Darkest were the rainy days in which blunt shadows fell grayly down the hall, the movement of wind-flicked trees outside the window causing knobbed silhouettes to ripple like volcanic smoke around the sockets and light switch. And as autumn progressed, the daytime darkness grew more frequent, seeming to mimic the rapidly plummeting mood of the house.

Eliman listened. When he heard no movement, he soldiered toward the kitchen.

Two years now, mornings had been for 'free reading,' meaning Eliman should stick to his room and shut the hell up. Instruction took place only in the afternoons. His mother's schedule. She was not an early riser. And without his father around she awoke even later. She often missed lunch these days, and Eliman made himself a bologna sandwich. He ate it at the table with a different book in his lap (there were morning books—books to be read in the privacy of his room—and there were afternoon books, overly simple, selected to please his mother).

Halfway through his sandwich she shuffled into the kitchen. Her hips had widened in the past six months and her jeans were too tight. She wore a wrinkled T-shirt. She hadn't showered. Her hair was still greasy and tangled in a ponytail.

"Get out," she said.

He set down the book, a Junie B. Jones, and made certain to place it on the table face up so she'd see the cover.

"I'm not done with my sandwich," he said.

"You get out now," she said flatly. "Take the sandwich. We'll start your lessons a little late today."

"What time?"

"Later. Or maybe we'll skip it. Maybe today's a holiday."

"Early Thanksgiving?" he said.

"Sure. Go be thankful."

He left the kitchen and set his sandwich on the coffee table.

Minutes later the mailbox made its tinny *perklunk*. He opened the door as James the mailman was walking away.

"Thank you!" Eliman shouted.

James held up a hand.

For good measure, in case his mother was listening, Eliman added, "Toast with jam! Got it!"

He brought in the envelopes and accordioned them across the coffee table next to his sandwich. None were from his father, which always came from Marrakesh in heavy FedEx sleeves with bar codes on their sides. Amid the pile, one of the envelopes, a simple off-white, was addressed incorrectly. Eliman walked it out to the sidewalk. He shivered in the stiff wind. Facing his own porch, he looked left to the house beside theirs. The dull gray numbers on the envelope matched the black, serifed plastic ones screwed next to its front door.

The letter was hers. The woman. His heart beat in his stomach, in his feet. It played the coarse rhythm of natural disasters: the break of storm-waves on the rocks, the angry assault of lightning. Eliman became a landslide, a thousand-ton avalanche snapping trees—one-two, one-two, just like that until the earth threatened to spin out of its orbit.

He read her name.

Lillian Damascine.

"What are you doing?" he said.

"Lillian," he said.

•　　•　　•

That night his father called for the first time in two weeks. His mother's voice from the living room was music echoing down a hallway.

"It's your dad," she said and handed the phone to Eliman. She kept hovering until he said, "Mom, is it okay if I talk to dad in private? Just for a minute?"

He held himself very still. She was forcing a smile, but there were times, times like this, when her carefully constructed expression disintegrated. Her complexion would grow ashen then. Times like these, the darkness slid immediately into the hollows of her face. The living room became a vacuum, without air or noise. And if Eliman took a breath, the change in compression would make his lungs explode.

This time she hesitated only slightly. The false smile kept its shape.

"Sure, hon." She walked out.

"El-dog!" his father said. "What up, big man? Tell me, how are things?"

Eliman had much to tell his father. His mother cried for two, sometimes three, hours a night. She washed her clothes in the bathtub because she said there were orcs in the basement behind the washer. Eliman hadn't been given a computer, but he had a library card and was allowed to walk the four blocks some days when his mother was chewing on washcloths and pacing that ragged path at the foot of her bed. At the library the woman at the desk told him orcs were from Tolkien. He read *The Hobbit* and the subsequent trilogy within a week, always in the mornings before leaving his room.

He wanted to tell his father that his mother had lost track of his, Eliman's, progress. She'd begun presenting him with first-grade readers and even kindergarten-level math books that she ordered out of the Christian catalog by the dozen. The first time he corrected her—to tell her he was far, far beyond Level 3 worksheets—she threw a chair through the sliding glass door leading onto the backyard. Later, she walked out shoeless to pick the prismatic little shards out of the weeds. Her feet bled, and Eliman fetched her the peroxide, which she poured into a pedicure tub. She'd cried then, too. And for the next three days Eliman prepared her meals and delivered them on a TV tray.

He'd learned to make soup this way.

Eliman said none of this to his father. He said, "Do you know the lady across from us?"

"Across the street? That's—what's her name—Hernandez. Mrs. Hernandez."

"No. Beside us."

"Oh. You mean Lilly."

"Yeah."

His father grew quiet. There was a very long pause. Eliman could hear him breathing strangely. His father shifted and it made a sound, the sound of movement on the other side of the world. His father was in a hotel surrounded by sand and mosques and people wearing headscarves.

Finally his father said, "Maybe don't bother her, El. I can't go into it, but maybe just—"

"We got her mail by accident."

"Did you give it to her?"

"Not yet."

"I wouldn't worry too much about it. Probably junk. Unless it's handwritten. Is it handwritten? Anyway, I thought you were going to ask me about your mom's birthday. I thought that's why you made her leave the room. It's November ninth, remember?"

Eliman felt that airless quality come over the room. He sensed his mother just outside the door or maybe listening in on the line.

"Look," said his father, "just don't say anything. There's a special package coming. I want you to follow the instructions. Don't let your mom see. Got it?"

Eliman nodded.

"Got it?"

"Yes, sir."

"Good boy. And get that mail back to Lil. Drop it in her mailbox. Don't talk to her, okay?"

A woman's voice bubbled up out of the background on his father's end. The voice had a gritty—what Eliman thought of as dirty—quality to it. It was deep and he heard his father's name.

"Bud, I have a meeting, so I have to go."

"Me, too," Eliman said.

"You have a meeting?" His father chuckled. "I miss you, buddy. Tell your mom I love her."

He was gone.

• • •

That night Eliman slept with Lillian Damascine's letter under his pillow. The address *was* handwritten. The envelope curved into the shape of his hand and he awoke once and felt the ripples in the paper beneath his thumb. He went back to sleep this way.

In the morning he found his mother on the kitchen floor, a line of drool dried down the side of her cheek. She still breathed. Eliman stepped over her to reach his cereal bowl. He envisioned himself as Thorondor, king of the Eagles, and floated to the refrigerator for milk. He turned back toward the table and stared at her. She wore the same T-shirt from yesterday and nothing else. She'd rolled to her stomach and he could see her wide buttocks, pale and dimpled and bare. He stared at it a long while and wondered if Lillian Damascine's ass looked like that. Probably not.

Lillian hadn't appeared in the window that morning, and Eliman had written 'NO' in dark, hard-carved lines that threatened to break through to the next page.

He poured his milk, and his mother still didn't move. He scooped up a fresh spoonful of Cheerios and held it out beyond the table. Again the room emptied of air. He turned over the spoon. The milk and seven Cheerios dropped and splattered flat across his mother's left rump. The Cheerios made a sound like *plop-plop-plop* and the milk ran down the back of her thigh and out onto the floor. Eliman dabbed up the dribble on the linoleum with his sock.

He waited in the living room. When James arrived, Eliman swung open the door. James nodded to Eliman from the other side of the screen.

"Wait," Eliman said.

"You have a package?"

James had dark skin. Eliman wanted to ask him if a black man and a white woman marrying was anything like trying to get an Avari to marry a dwarf, which almost made him laugh. But he apparently thought about this too long, because James said, "Hello in there?"

"Huh?"

James looked at Eliman like he was simple. Eliman recognized that look.

"I'm not stupid," Eliman said.

"Do you have a package?"

"My mom fell in the kitchen. She's in the kitchen."

"Is she okay?"

"She's not awake."

James reached for the handle on the screen door and stopped.

"Is there somebody you could call? I'm not really supposed to."

"My dad isn't in the country. He's in Morocco looking for oil."

"Oil? Is your mom in there or not?"

"My mom," Eliman said. "Not my dad."

James looked twice down the street and finally stepped off the porch. Eliman watched him go.

He went back into the living room and thought about checking on his mom. Then he thought about getting *The Silmarillion* out of his room to read in the sugary amber sunlight sliding down over the soft slope of the couch in front of the window with the blue and red afghan resting warm there and calling him. He scratched his knee. Then the screen door rattled and this made Eliman think of how he'd left open the main door and about how there was an edge to the breeze sliding over the false flowers in the vase in the hallway and how the cold air was stealing up the stairs and across the broad ceiling with the shapes in the stucco-like plaster, the ceiling with its violent swirls his father had made with a brush to give it texture that made secret signs in the whiteness and that looked down on Eliman sometimes as he lay on the floor looking up, and in the plaster there were monster mouths and hideous things dying in the boiling-up melting world and then he would blink and they were gone.

The screen door rattled again.

"You still there, kid?"

Eliman walked to the door and saw James standing there with Lillian Damascine. She wore a yellow button-up top and white jeans. Her hips were thinner than his mother's, and her shirt was unbuttoned low. The skin at the top of her chest seemed darker than the color of her back in the mornings. It was the first time he'd seen her face. She'd grown eyes and a roundish nose and naturally pink lips, a very light shade, and she said, "Do you know me? I'm your neighbor. I'm Lillian."

Eliman pushed open the door. She stepped into the house with James. Eliman pointed down the hallway.

She reached the kitchen and said, "Oh god," then stepped over Eliman's mother.

James kneeled beside her and touched his mother's shoulder. He felt for a pulse in her neck. He said "She has cereal on her ass," and pointed.

"Help me," Lillian said. She took a dish towel that had been hanging across the faucet. As they turned her over, she spread the towel across Eliman's mother's lap like it was a napkin for a person at a fancy restaurant. The towel covered up the place where his mother's underwear should have been, and James looked away.

His mother woke up.

"Barbara," Lillian said, "are you okay? Can you talk."

His mother brushed the springy brown hair out of her face. It fell back. "What are you doing here?"

"We came."

Barbara's eyes cleared. She frowned and talked through her teeth. "Get out of my house."

"Your son."

She looked at Eliman and said, "He can go, too."

Then James spoke, and whatever metal wire, invisible and hot, that had been strung between the two women and the boy was cut. "Be reasonable," he said. "You've had an episode."

"An episode?"

"Are you epileptic?"

"It's booze," she said.

"It's not," he said. He sniffed the air.

"I got shitfaced," she said.

"Don't kid yourself. The boy was scared. Do you have medication?"

Eliman's mother laughed. She laughed like a big fat clown in a circus. The sound filled the room from cupboards to coffee pot. She searched around on the floor and came up with an orange pill bottle. "I got all the medication I need."

"I'm calling the police," James said.

"Oh, stop it. It wasn't like that."

"The hell it wasn't," he said quietly.

"Hell it wasn't."

"Where's your husband?" Lillian said.

"You know he's out of the country. Don't act like you don't."

"I have to get back to work," James said. He stood up and wiped his hands on his pants like he'd been working in a garden. "I'm calling the police."

Barbara opened her mouth and made a face like Eliman

had never seen her make, like she'd scream and burst. It was different from her face when she threw her fits. Now her cheeks got very red, and there were white blotches under her eyes. "God, I don't—don't get the police into this. Can't you see—"

· "Will you let me check on you this evening?" Lillian said.

"Anything." Tears rolled down her cheeks. They weren't like the tears Eliman imagined when he heard her crying in the dark behind the door of her room. The tears in the kitchen were long, slender, icicle-like things that rolled down her flattened face in snaky little streams.

"I'll check on her, okay?" Lillian said to James.

James took a step toward the door. "It's on you."

Eliman's mother pointed at him.

"Take him," she said to Lillian.

"You're not going to do anything stupid, right?"

"Take him," she said. She handed Lillian the orange bottle. "I'll get cleaned up. I just need a little time, maybe I'll go to the grocery store."

"I can go."

"No. Just take him."

Lillian touched Eliman's shoulder and led him out of the kitchen. "Just for the afternoon."

He was allowed to retrieve his book, and on the way out he found the package James had left on the porch. It sat beneath the wicker chair to the right of the door.

It was from his father.

•   •   •

He heard Lillian speaking to his mother over the phone.

"Yes yes, I'll be sure. You rest up."

The windows had all dimmed into twilight as he spent the afternoon reading, sitting on Lillian Damascine's starch-stiff couch with the wood whorls in the arms and the paisley flowers spreading like teardrops over a field of golden-green. Thorondor, king of the Eagles, had just slashed Morgoth's eyes and successfully returned the body of Fin-golfin, High King of the elves, to its rightful burial place as the sun in Charityburg turned to ash.

Eliman looked up to see Lillian standing in the doorway staring at him.

"You know," she said. "I promise I'm not a bad person."

"I don't think you're bad." He blinked. His sullen, calm eyes were unmoved and unrevealing.

"Well, you haven't spoken to me all afternoon. You've just been reading. You haven't even gone to the bathroom."

"Mom says I should be quiet around adults."

"About that," she said. "About your mom. She really needs a night to herself. It's up to you, but are you okay sleeping here?"

A helium-light bubble of nausea filled Eliman's stomach. He had to urinate pretty bad, and the combined feeling of pressure and weightlessness turned to warm blood flow between his legs.

"I have to go to the bathroom."

● ● ●

Much later, in Lillian's guest bedroom on the first floor, Eliman tried to situate himself so the crack in the door gave him a view of the stairs. He could just make out the heavily painted banister and the buffed wooden steps with the old smell—the smell of an aging house, of old wood, dignified but clean. Lillian had been in her bathrobe when she ascended those stairs. Her robe was the color of Easter bunnies.

Finally he sat up. His bare feet touched the smooth black floor. Everything here was smooth and pristine and polished. The cleanliness gave him a sense of order. He swiped his feet over the wood and listened to the dry sound they made. Then he rose and he switched on the lamp. On top of a small round table rested the unopened package from his father, slightly bigger than a shoe box.

Inside were several items. On top was a birthday card. An attached sticky-note said, "Eliman, sign this." Across the front of the card were the words *Feliz Cumpleaños!!* On the inner blank section his father had written, "Hang in there, baby! We got plenty good years left to celebrate! Happy B-day! —J"

Eliman set it aside.

Four smaller boxes, all wrapped in the same silver paper, were nested in packing material made of shredded cardboard. Another note, stuck to the largest one, said, "Eliman, Get up early on your mom's birthday and put these on the kitchen table before she comes downstairs. If you can buy yellow roses, put those with them."

Written directly on the wrapping paper of one gift were the words, "Special: Open Later." Eliman lifted it out and carried it to the cot where he picked at the transparent tape. He freed it, pried up the carefully folded edges, and slid the box out. The box was roughly textured in an expensive way with Arabic lettering scrolled flamboyantly across the top. Eliman lifted the lid. Neatly folded inside were two silky bunches. He held them up. One was underwear, the other a bra, both a deep shade of turquoise with black lacy trim. They felt like nothing between his fingers.

Before he lost his nerve, he stood up and tiptoed out into the hall. He climbed the stairs. The solid old wood didn't creak. Lillian's door had been left open. The faint light of the moon, its blue essence sullen and calm, stretched over the frost-white bed, the soft curves of the chair, the lamps and featureless walls.

Lillian lay on her back, her mouth slightly open. Her bare shoulders were visible above the blanket. Eliman thought about what might happen if he were to pull back the covers very quickly, what he would see, even if only for a moment. He stood very close to her, watching her breathe. She exhaled and he drew it deep inside him. He tasted the warmth in his lungs. Then he moved away in the dark, in the quiet, and found the drawer where she kept her undergarments. They seemed ghostly to his eyes under the moonlight. He folded his mother's silken things and placed them at the back of the drawer.

going anywhere

Without looking back, he retreated downstairs, wadded the paper into a silver ball, light as a bird, and hid it behind the cot. He slept soundly after that.

• • •

The next morning Lillian made pancakes on an electric griddle. He could smell the fruity shampoo rising off her wet hair and mixing with the sweetness of the pancakes as she moved about the kitchen.

"Are you going to have coffee?" he said.

"Don't tell me your mom lets you drink coffee."

"Sometimes. When I feel like it."

"I don't really drink it."

Something had changed about her tone. He wanted to argue—yes, she did. She did drink coffee. It was another smell, another detail he held from his time at the window. It crossed the space between them, touched him, turned him sideways every morning. Why lie about that?

"I'm sure your mom is dying to see you," she said. She slid him another short stack.

"I don't know."

"Don't mistake it," she said. "Your mom is going through some stuff."

He felt hurt. They'd talked like friends for a moment last night. 'Are you okay sleeping here?' she'd said. The decision had been his, and she'd wanted him to stay, and he'd wanted her to find the lacy things in the morning.

But now he was a child again. She stirred the batter, and Eliman was a child.

• • •

She delivered him home. In the living room was a large woman in a black blazer. She and his mother were sipping tea and speaking quietly.

His mother wore a summer dress, too light for the weather. It clung to her hips and bunched oddly beneath her breasts. The front of it sagged out like a paunch. But she'd

62

washed her hair, and the smell was a little like Lillian's.

The large woman rested a clipboard on her lap and beckoned Eliman.

"What's your name?" Her breath smelled of food—onions and steak and butter.

"Eliman," he said.

"That's an interesting name."

He shrugged.

"Where does it come from? Do you know?"

"It's a homophone," he said.

"I don't know what that is, honey."

"It's when a word sounds like something else. My middle name is Opal."

"Opal," she repeated. "That's another interesting name."

"Sure," he said.

"What's that have to do with a homophone?"

"Opal—the nickname is Opie, like in that show."

She grinned widely. A spot of lipstick was on her front tooth. He thought about how his mother had been staring at that gob of scab-red lipstick all morning.

"Opie," the woman said. "Oh, I love that show. Andy Griffith." She started to whistle.

"It's a *hidden* homophone," Eliman said. "That's what mom calls it. My mom is smart." He hadn't thought about whether or not he believed this. But he did. He'd forgotten it, but he did. His mother was smart. Just broken. And that's why this woman had come. Not because his mother was smart, but because smart sometimes made you break, and then someone had to check on you.

"A hidden homophone," the woman repeated.

"Eliman Opie," he said.

It took the woman a long while, but her new expression, puzzled and inscrutable, erupted slowly, like an earthquake taking up all the features of her face and jostling them around so that he couldn't tell if she were smiling or squinching or having a stroke. Maybe it was a seizure like James the mailman had said about his mother.

"I get it," she said softly, no smile. She wrote something down on her clipboard.

His mother leaned forward.

"Words make up everything," she explained. Her back had gone stiff. "Letters make up words. Eliman is the center of the alphabet. He's the middle of it, the foundation for everything. It means something to us, Jason and I."

The big woman dismissed Eliman.

• • •

For the next three days he waited to see if Lillian would appear at her window in the new lingerie. She didn't. She didn't appear at all. He spent the hours of those days in his room, cloistered with the *Silmarillion*, reading it slowly so as not to run out of the words. After the big woman left, his mother had closed herself in her bedroom. She'd covered all her windows in duct tape. She'd dragged in six lamps from other parts of the house and removed the lampshades. The brilliant white bulbs surrounded her like an honor guard.

Eliman checked on her in the evenings. Always in the same position, she was curled against her headboard, half-slumped into a rumpled stack of pillows, all the light burning, robbing the room of corners.

In those three days, the Balrog and the orcs fell. Morgoth made one last assault. Thorondor countered again, aided by Eärendil with his white flame. The sun and the moon turned the hard and soft shadows like pages of a book. And as he read, Eliman listened to the sounds of the neighborhood transformed into battle-axes broken against the long brilliant shields of vanquishers, shouts high on a distant hill, the rush of leathern feet building into thunder on the plains.

• • •

On the morning of his mother's birthday, Eliman left his room early. He showered. He placed the three presents on the kitchen table in a silver tableau. The opalescent bows shimmered in the sunlight. He found flowers in the back-yard, late-blooming yellow dandelions with coarse stems and rigid leaves that felt good and rough in his hands. He imagined clutching the leathery hilt of Ringil, sword of Fin-golfin, that steely cold spark, the weight of it as he thrust it forward. He returned to the kitchen, breathing deeply, ready. He placed the dandelions in a soup can filled with water and spread them out in a respectable arrangement.

But then his bravery failed. Instead of going to his moth-er's room, he retreated to his own. He held his mother's birthday card and looked out his window again for Lillian.

She'd abandoned him.

He felt sick. Unable to continue.

"Just once," he said. He wanted to see her again, either in the underthings or out of them.

He'd give anything.

He retrieved her envelope from beneath his pillow. It had been warped by its several nights in his hands. He opened it. It was a letter on stiff paper, handwritten:

Lil,

Sorry it's been three days since my last letter. Maybe I should switch to email, but that robs this thing we have of something—plus, is easily snooped. More problems off the coast with exploration at Cap Rhir—two divers lost for a few hours, then threat of government inspection for safety. Not to mention spending all my time trapsing (?) up and down the coast and arguing with officials in Rha-bat. Don't know why they put me up here in Andalou if I'm never here. Oh well. Not what I was meaning to say. Boring stuff.

I think of you always. Dream of your ———. You can fill in. All would be true. The tongue knows. You said that, right? Or was it me. Either way, I'm doing poorly with say-

ing something special to express how I'm feeling these days: here's an honest effort:

You are flames. You are burning and brilliant. You are the wind roaring in from the open ocean. You are more to me than the rest of the world. If all other things crumble to ruin, you are still—you are everything, and just a bit more.

Love love love forever,

J

Eliman's veins went cold copper. He touched his teeth with his tongue. In the kitchen he could hear his mother.

• • •

He found her seated at the table, arms and upper body sprawled out, face flat on a placemat. All the presents were torn open as if they'd each, in succession, burst free on their own. A black fountain pen had popped out of one box, while a pair of pearl earrings in gold settings, and a gold brooch in the guise of a ruby-eyed frog, had spilled forth from the other two.

She wasn't crying.

"Mom?"

"Time to go away now," she said.

"Mom."

"There's no love here," she said. She half rose and held up the pen, the earrings, the frog. She let them drop onto the table.

"Mom," he said, and handed her the birthday card. In ink, in the cold empty inner flap, was his father's note, the one telling her to hang in there. On the other side, beneath the printed reiteration of *Feliz Cumpleaños!!*, Eliman had written in his strongest, his most severe hand, his darkest pencil, a message:

Mom,

You are brilliant. You are the wind. You are more to me than the rest of the world. If other things crumble, you are still everything, and just a bit more.

Love love love,

Eliman

The first of her smiles was a broken one. The struggle, Eliman saw, was immense. But he held his breath and her smile came, and it was genuine. She flattened the card and felt the imprint of his writing as if she were reading braille.

"God, that's nice," she said. She wasn't quite looking his way, but her new smile was holding. "You're so smart."

He put his hand on the table next to hers, not touching her but waiting. She half stood, then sat, surveyed the table, and noticed his dandelions.

"I didn't even hear the doorbell," she said.

"What?" he said. The room felt like glass.

"The doorbell. The florist must have delivered these early." She drew in a deep whiff of the dandelions and cupped her hands around the can, lifting them slowly to fluff the blossoms. "They're perfect."

She still hadn't looked at him.

"How perfect and small and clean," she said.

His hand was waiting on the table.

•　•　•

I head south. The wilderness rolls. Immense evergreens flow in waves beneath me. My shadow makes a double-bladed knife that ripples across whole swaths, blots out the sun for woodland animals a moment, then is gone. That darkness feels heavy as if even now I carry with me the weight of evil from the land to the north.

Morgoth is defeated.

I am Thorondor, king of the eagles, victor, talons loose,

67

wind lifting my outstretched wings obediently. And to the south, beyond the trees of Dorthonion, beyond the river Sirion and the lands of the Sindar, beyond the bleak blue Ered Luin range, there is Eliman of the new earth, where a plotted run of square homes edge against one another in the flat sparkling settlement of Ohio.

Eliman. The middle of everything known. Victor.

•   •   •

The first of her smiles was at the kitchen table, that was true.

The fifth and seventh—the unconstructed, the organic, grins—came two weeks later from jokes he made. Fifteen and twenty-eight evolved into full-on laughs. The forty-third made her snort soda out of her nose.

Eliman recorded them for weeks, these smiles. He watched the window in the mornings and, when Lillian Damascine didn't show, he tended to his mother. He soared the yard in wonder at his own power, looking down among the blades as he collected flowers in the afternoons. Sometimes he resorted to hardy berry stems from rigid shrubs nestled against the patch of woods behind the house. He swept down on them. And he kept up his courting, recognizing in it his own strength. He left her notes in the windowsill over the sink, small, insignificant things no bigger than fortune-cookie papers, sometimes with only one word: beautiful, the best, generous, caring, smart smart smart. Until she returned the favor one day by surprising him with a small book on his bed: *Tree and Leaf* by J.R.R. Tolkien—a book the library didn't possess and for which he'd put a request into the circulation desk weeks ago.

She slowly returned the lamps to their rightful places. The evenings took on their old shapes. Soft shadows bloomed, quiet, while the two of them read, alone together, in their separate chairs, occasionally glancing upward to see the other one, still sitting, still engrossed or not, but not broken.

courier

The barcoded packages came less frequently.

There was a divorce.

A year. A whole year went by.

Then there was the night when he saw his father dancing with Lillian in her kitchen. Eliman held back the cold curtain—it was early spring—and he watched them laughing in sing-songy ways that sounded too harsh, too forced. She wore the turquoise night things, and Eliman watched them. His father hadn't called to say he was back in the country.

The morning after that, for the first time in a very long time, through the pale swoon of mist webbing the grass, Eliman watched Lillian Damascine sit at the table with her naked back to him. The steam of her coffee rose over her shoulder. That scent crossed the lawn.

The morning took shape, and Eliman waited. The world was silent, and he waited. To see her. While the early doves darted over the space between them, shooting shadows across the grass, Eliman waited. For a chance to see her nakedness full and untouched in the morning. And he waited—maybe to see, just, if she were smiling or not.

bethesda

You are eight and trembling in the morning cold, despite the fact it's summer. The sun hasn't risen yet, and as I lift you out of the car I wait for you to wake. You open your eyes slowly. A father and his son, we both stare at the already filling parking lot of the public pool. It's disheartening, this many people, the headlights winking out, the darkness turning the cars immediately into soft-edged shapes with muted colors. I'd hoped word wasn't out yet, that we were somehow the first to hear.

The people are wordless as they walk up the concrete ramp where a mist folds back from the old wooden gate. The gate is padlocked at night in an attempt to keep teens from slipping in for midnight swims. But that's all the security there is at night.

Now a young lifeguard, a girl with short blonde hair, is unlocking and removing the chain. She is slight in a brilliant red one-piece, and she's all the security there is in the morning. We live in a small town, in Ohio you know, and maybe it's a community thing or a Midwestern thing,

bethesda

but the crowds are still civil. Each car is packed with a million hopes—for cures and relief mostly, but some for other things—and someday, I hate to say, you'll realize what some people will do to get what they want. You'll realize how much bigger the world is than what we have now.

I set you gently down in a standing position so you can lean against the car. I position your feet a little wider than your shoulders to help you with your balance. You rub your eyes.

"Crutches," you say.

"Chair," I say. "Willie, we talked about this. The wait could be a while. All day, maybe."

"I want to walk."

"Fine," I say. "But I'm bringing the chair. You'll thank me."

I know what you're thinking. You don't want the chair because it doesn't fit the scene. You're like that. You remember last year when we went to the beach and I made the mistake of assuming I could roll you down to the surf, but the wheels sunk immediately into the soft, brown sand, and I swore a little and finally carried you to your beach towel beside your mother. Then later I took you into the water, and you wouldn't wave back to her because you could see the chair behind her, mired like a washed-up medical apparatus that reminds everyone there's a real and un-wonderful world out there. That was my fault: I'd drawn attention to the chair with my outburst, and now everyone who passed by looked around or didn't, but the chair was a blight. It didn't belong, and maybe this made you think the same thing about yourself, that maybe you didn't deserve a day at the beach. All I know is you wouldn't look back at your mother, and I knew it was because of the chair.

• • •

You're pretty good crossing the parking lot. You're shaking off the stiffness, and you've got that morning burst of energy. You're smiling. Moments like this I try, for a second, to

71

see you as other people do. The small frame, knees buckled inward, baggy jeans and a T-shirt two sizes too large, making you look younger than the other boys your age. You get talked down to a lot, and the way your mom cut your hair, straight across, with the downy blonde making you seem even more childish, that doesn't help. I hang back with the wheelchair just to watch you, because you're not a little kid anymore. I'm proud the way you don't look back at me.

Then there's the concrete ramp up to the entrance. It's wide enough for a car, and the people passing us give you room. You're slowing down, and I'm ready to throw out an arm if someone comes too close to the crutches. You've fallen before like that. There was the busted lip and the chipped tooth when we were in line to see Santa at the Easton Mall.

This makes me think of that dog. I've never told you this, but it was when I first moved out. When I was twenty. I inherited a dog from my parents, your grandma and granddad. It was a small dog they were going to take to the pound because it wouldn't stop pissing on the rug. I took it because I didn't want to see it killed, but I could never get it house-trained. Sometimes I hit it I was so angry.

I'm not proud of that.

There are times I want to tell you about that dog because I want you to know how awful it made me feel afterward. He was black and white and long-eared, named Perkins, Perk for short, and he couldn't have weighed more than six pounds. I'd slap him on the head and tell myself I was disciplining, punishing with purpose. The dog, in his fright, would crouch, and another yellow puddle would form on the carpet beneath him, and that would only make me angrier. I'd hit him again.

Afterward, after I'd cooled down, the dog would curl against me on the couch while I watched television.

Maybe I really only want to tell you this because there are times when you make me so frustrated. There's an anger in me, and it's a barbed thing, and sometimes I want to shake you out of your sickness.

bethesda

Maybe times like now, watching you on the ramp, it's easier for me to say this because I'm further from myself, I'm further from the pain in you, I'm further from Perk, and there's hope in the *us*.

Maybe I just want you to grow up to be a man I can talk to.

•   •   •

We pass the concession stand and even though you don't say anything, I see you glance at the popcorn machine, dark and quiet now but ready to be filled with a puffy and buttery whiteness. I'm already planning on getting you some, then you turn to me and ask, "Where?"

I look around the pool. It's L-shaped. The shallow end directly in front of us is the top of the L, while the lower end to our right is comprised of the swimming lanes. My heart sinks to see so many people already claiming their spots on the dew-dark grass, most of them near the shallows. A few have staked claim near the separate kiddie pool, a small square with its own green fence. There isn't much room inside that fence, and there's no grass like around the main pool, so some people have set up lawn chairs. They're holding infants mostly, but also there's an old man and his wife. He's stretched himself out on a threadbare beach towel over the concrete, and his wife is knelt over him stroking his hair back from his head.

I know we have to act decisively, but this is for you.

"Where do you want to wait?" I ask. "Got a good feeling?"

I can tell you're worried about the congestion of people surrounding the shallow end, even though jumping in on that side is obviously safer. I see that look of apprehension you get when we're at the matinee on those rare days we get out of the hospital early, when the day-blind crowd is trundling in through the doors and searching for seats. With the movies, I try to have you there early most times, but it doesn't always work out. Sometimes, if it's the first show, the theater doesn't open until ten minutes before the movie starts. One time, even after we were seated, a middle-aged man in khakis and a polo shirt came in a few minutes after the movie had begun and tried to politely slide past us in the aisle. I couldn't get to your crutches in time, and he tripped on them and swore. It took him a moment to see what had happened, and when I said sorry, he said no, he was very sorry, there was no excuse. He felt badly, I could see, but the entire movie, I think, was ruined for you. I could see you holding those crutches until the credits. Instead of leaning them against the seat, you drew them close enough to be out of the walkway, but low enough to stay below the height of your head. You're considerate that way. You think of those things.

Not like me. I sometimes put the scene of me cursing on the beach alongside that man doing the same when he fell in the movie theater, and I wonder whose outburst was more justified. I tend to think it's his.

"Better hurry," I say.

You look around and finally point to a spot at the far end of the pool, way at the bottom of the L where the diving boards hover over the water from three different heights.

"All right," I say. "You want me to carry you in the chair?"

"I can do it."

You continue on with the crutches, though I can tell already that the ramp has momentarily taken a step out of your speed. By the time we reach the place where you pointed, a heavyset couple wrangling a two-year-old in nothing but a diaper have claimed it with a quilt. The toddler has burns up and down his legs and all across his chest up to the shoulders. A wide pink scar like a spill has pulled the skin over his left eye down into his cheek.

"Sorry, bud," I say to you.

"It's okay, Dad. That's a good spot. And they need it."

A few others have begun to claim the spots along the water, and I rush ahead of you to get what I can, squeezing past the couple and laying your chair on its side to claim as much of the empty space as possible. I look back and see

bethesda

you coming over the grass. The crutches make soft clicking sounds, and I think for a second how accustomed to that sound I've become, how much I even like it. It means you're coming. It means you've finished playing in the living room and are headed toward the kitchen for lunch. It means your mom is at work and because I'm the one at home now, I'm cooking you grilled cheese, I'm fixing tomato soup, and we're going to sit and talk. You're so smart. Everything you say lights me up, and that clicking sound is a sound I love.

Your mom thought coming here was a ridiculous idea. She said, "Don't get his hopes up, Ted." She told me I had to stop trying to squeeze miracles out of oddly shaped stones and four-leaf clovers. She told me it was all superstition.

All I could think to tell her was that I'd be ashamed if this whole thing with the pool turned out to be true and I hadn't tried. I told her I'd hate myself if I didn't at least give you a shot.

• • •

You navigate around the couple just as others begin to fill in behind you. The place is thronging now, even though the early dark still gives them a quiet and hazy quality like a Seurat painting. Morning by the pool.

I upend the chair and lay out our two beach towels side-by-side only to find that I've chosen our position poorly. We're way at the bottom-right tip of the L, and our angle toward the water is oblique. We only have a shot at the corner of the pool. The diving board platforms are too close. If any more people come, the platforms will create congestion and close off an avenue. We'll be boxed out. I look for any other spot, but the grass along the concrete has become a continuous row of blankets and bags and towels and people. I'm tempted to edge onto the concrete surrounding the pool, but I've heard the rules, same as all these other people apparently. Nothing happens if anyone is on the walkway. Some people say that's why it never happens in the kiddie pool. Because there is no grass there. There's no boundary to ensure a distance between the people and the water.

"I'm sorry," I say as you lower yourself onto our towel.

"It's okay, Dad. This is a good spot. It's a straight shot." You sight with your arm the corner of the pool toward which we'll be running. I'm already positioning myself behind and slightly to the right of you so that I can hook you under your armpits and toss you forward. We've been practicing this at about half speed. Last night I spent two hours throwing you onto our queen-size mattress, which I'd dragged onto the living room floor. You laughed the whole time. But I'm rethinking that exercise. My arms are tired, and I'd never forgive myself if the fact that I loved the sound of your giggling made me practice an hour too long, if it made me lose a crucial burst of speed today.

"Trunks?" I say.

You scan the crowd. You're wearing those baggy jeans that are a little too long. They trip you up sometimes, but you've started to be self-conscious about your legs. Your legs are thin and the calves are straighter than most kids your age. You've somehow figured this out, and maybe that doesn't surprise me. Like I said, you think of those things. You notice.

"Wait until nobody's looking," you say.

"Nobody's looking now."

You point to a woman with down syndrome who is staring at us from across the eight lanes of water. She's waving to you. You wave back and smile. She smiles. Then an elderly woman takes her by the arm and leads her away from the water's edge, toward a yellow and black afghan that reminds me of Charlie Brown's shirt.

"Now," you say.

I'm ready. I toss a beach towel over your legs. I unbutton your jeans, and you pull the towel up to your chest. We've practiced this maneuver too, though far longer than the mattress-diving. This is something you learn from early on because of the potty issues. We've got the change down to a science. I move my hands to the bottom of the towel and shove them all the way under like I'm birthing a cow. I find the tops of your jeans and the elastic of your underwear and pull them out from under your butt. Then they're off and tossed aside, and I've pushed the trunks, even the elastic inner underwear, over your feet and up. I lift you a little and get them to your waist.

"Can you tie the string?" I say.

You nod. I start to pull up the towel covering your legs, but you lay a hand across your lap. "Can we leave it?"

"You sure?" I say. "Nobody's going to be looking. I promise. Nobody will even notice. Your legs are fine."

You look like you're thinking it over.

"Just for a while," you say. "Maybe I'll take it off later."

"Okay, buddy."

You have some trouble with the drawstring of your swimming trunks, even though I picked these out special. The string is thick and white, more like rope, and threaded through two brass eyelets on the outside of the trunks instead of the inside of the waistband. It's stylistic, these little differences. I know that. But for you it's functional. The larger string makes all the difference in the world, and I'm proud because you've been practicing. You finish about the fifth attempt, never making a peep of frustration. In that moment I'm admiring you. You're the strongest person I know.

"Ready to take off the towel, get a little suntan?" I say.

You give a side-to-side glance of the pool's perimeter and nod your head. "Sure. Okay."

I pull it off of you and your legs are lying there on the towel like two fish. The doctor said there'll come a point where they'll be more of a hindrance to you than a boon. He said that, but I still see you walking one day. I still see you running down a hill, feeling the speed of abandon as you rush toward me, your arms outstretched. We've still got that chance, you and I, because of the pool.

I layer some sunscreen over your shins, lift your bare feet and give your toes a peck.

"Daa-aa-d," you say.

"Sorry. I'm embarrassing you. You're too old for that."

"That's okay, Dad." And I'm proud of you all over again because you can see kissing your toes means something to me. I've done it since your first bath time, and you don't want to take it away from me. Not yet. You're smart and sensitive like that, and I'm frustrated all over again that a cure isn't judged on character, because you're the best. You're the one person out here that deserves a break.

"You ready for this?" I say.

"Ready steady," you say.

"I got water in the cooler, and a couple sandwiches."

Just then a crack of high-pitched music stabs the silence. I turn and see a couple teenagers with a portable stereo—I didn't even know they made those anymore. There's a CD slot in the top.

"You mind turning that off?" I say.

A girl with dyed black hair and a nose ring stares back at me. She's wearing athletic shorts over a purple swimsuit.

"It's Christian music," she says.

"I don't care it's Christian music. It's awful. Nobody wants it on."

She looks around and there are other people staring at her. The music is still going. It's Alice-Cooper-knock-off-rock with words about Jesus in all the places Alice would say something about feeling disenfranchised and angry. The other people around us are staring out of the corners of their eyes. They're staring at the young man she's with, too, whose hair is also dyed black. He's skinny in a way she'll never be, and she probably hates him for it.

"Fine," she says. She turns it down.

"Turn it off," I say. Something about being your dad, it's made me more aggressive. I notice this occasionally. I don't take shit from people. About a year ago I started doing push-ups in the mornings. In the evenings, too. I started running when I could get away. That's something I never used to do. Feeling stronger makes me feel better equipped. And

78

I know I'll throw an elbow if this girl or her boyfriend tries to get past us.

She cuts the music and says something under her breath, but I let it go. A calm ripples out over the crowd again. This isn't a place for music. It's not. You're holding your ears, and I pull your hands down.

"It's all right," I say. "It's off."

You lean in to me and whisper. "I didn't like that."

"It's Christian rock, buddy. Nobody does."

I worry the girl will say something about your legs or your wheelchair to get back at me, and I think about how I could punch a teenage girl in the face if she said something like that. I'm already making a fist, and veins are standing out on my knuckles.

• • •

A few hours in and the sun climbs and the air warms. We're in for a long one, you and me. People are flipping themselves over on towels and blankets, baking brown and waiting. The old man by the kiddie pool has begun to moan, and it lends an edge to the mood. One of the pool staff asks if they shouldn't call an ambulance and I hear the old woman tell her no. No, they'll just take a glass of ice water if the staff can spare it.

The girl says they have to charge for ice water, but the woman has no money.

Someone gives the girl a dollar. She looks relieved and fetches it. She brings back a bag of chips, too.

You watch some of this, and sometimes you stare at the water. You're not looking at me, and I wonder why. You tend to feel bad, I know, about the impositions you put on people, but I wish I could make you understand this is my place, this is the most important spot for me. There's nothing else in the world.

"Will it be soon, Dad?"

"We don't know, buddy."

"I mean till the popcorn is ready."

I lean out to try and get a read on the concession stand, but it's blocked by the line of shower stalls and the entrances to the men's and women's locker rooms.

"Might be a little while."

"I smell it."

"Maybe not, then, I guess."

"Can I have some?"

"Of course." But there's a problem. What if I miss our chance? What if the minute I walk away, there it is, the brilliant white light over the water, because it could come at any time or not at all, and everybody is charging forward to be the first in the pool because the first is the only one who matters, who gets healed, and you're stuck there, and all the mattress-diving and all the planning doesn't do us any good? I wish that girl who went and got the cup of ice would come this way. About now I'd pay her twenty dollars for a bag of popcorn.

You start to cry.

"Hey, Willie, what is it? What is it, buddy?"

"I'm sorry," you say. Your bottom lip is pulled down, and the edges of your eyes are red.

"Tell me what's wrong."

"I don't feel good." You look up, and I can see the down syndrome woman staring at you again from across the pool.

"Is it her?"

You shake your head. You plunge your face into your hands. Your fingers are doing that thing, the shaky thing. They're twitching over your eyebrows. You say something without lifting your mouth from your palm.

"What?" I say.

"She's looking at my legs. My legs hurt."

"Which is it? Do they hurt or not?" I can feel that old anger surging in my stomach, and suddenly I have the urge to grab either side of your mouth and pinch your face as hard as I can to shut you up. I want to shake you and make you strong, tell you to stop cry-babying, the way my dad did to me.

bethesda

I swallow it all down real slow.

I start rubbing your legs, but you cry harder. We're making a little scene, you and I.

I'm gritting my teeth, saying, "Keep it together, bud. You got to stop crying." The girl and her boyfriend behind us are looking, but their faces are flat and blank.

Finally I point across the pool at the down syndrome woman. "Is it her?"

I don't even wait for you to answer. I'm up before I can think, and I'm around the diving boards. I find the old woman and her husband. They're dressed the way old people dress. She's in a house dress. He's wearing a short-sleeve blue button-up and brown slacks. The pants are polyester. He's wearing brown shoes, and he's raising up. He's a short man, a stout man, maybe even a healthy man for his age, not like the old guy over at the kiddie pool.

"Is that your daughter?"

I point to the down syndrome woman.

"She's our granddaughter," says the old woman.

"Is it possible? Could you please? Could you have her stop staring at my son?"

The old woman gets to her feet, and she tugs on her granddaughter's arm. The down syndrome woman is thick as the old man with heavy glasses and a short haircut. She smiles at me, and I wave to her because I can't think of anything else.

I look at the old man. He's been asleep, definitely. This is not a thing he thought he'd be doing. Not coming to a public pool at his age, not taking care of his granddaughter for years and years, forever. It's not how he saw his life when he was twenty-five and standing at the altar with this woman, their hands coming together as the priest mumbled out scripture.

He's staring up at me, his hand visored across his forehead, and there is nothing left to say between us. I leave him there—my fists are clinched into hammers, and I swear I was ready to use them—and I jog for the concession stand.

81

going anywhere

The last I see of you, you're on the towel watching, and from here, from this far away, I can't tell you've been crying. God, I wish I could wish that away, that anxiety making me look, trying to tell if you're all right. Right now there's only your features and your absolutely dark eyes, and I'm thinking I can pretend. I can pretend your fine.

As I reach the concession stand I'm finally cooling down a little, sucking in shallow breaths between my teeth. I order a large popcorn and think about you. But now I'm crashing inside, I'm sliding low into some gray moment, and it's sending me way out there, bud. It's giving me a glimpse of a pitiless future all pain and nothing but heartache.

I usually keep the long-term visions, the future stuff, at bay until right before I drift off to sleep. They visit me then, and mostly I keep them above board, if you know what I mean. I look at all the opportunities you'll have, your college education, the way your brain will work and how you'll find ways to be better than me, ways I can't even imagine. And sometimes when I can't sleep because all those possibilities are floating out there, and every one of them is loud and difficult and sometimes angry and triumphant, and other times mottled in ugly shadows, when I can't sleep, I rise and look into your bedroom. And I can see on your face all the ways you struggled that day, all the times you hurt and were stared at, and in your sleep it's all slipping away for a little instant, and you're free, and I'm free, and you and me, we're free in the free dark world together where it's quiet and settled and done.

A shout rises up as I take the popcorn bag, and all my worst fears are realized. The crowd around the pool is surging toward the water. Someone has raised an infant over her head and been jostled by a man with one leg. He throws himself forward and claws at the concrete. There are screams and the smack of skin, the sweaty slap of limbs as the crowd converges. I've tossed the popcorn aside and I'm running. I'm running toward you, I swear, but I'm so far away at this point. I'm fighting. I push people out of my way. The splashing has begun, but I'm still hoping, maybe there's a loophole, that even after a hundred, a thousand, are in the water, you can still be chosen.

I spot you just as you lean over the edge of the pool. You're on your feet and your crutches are to the front and back of you in full stride like I've never seen before. Your pale knuckles have gone red you've got such a grip. I see the girl in the dark bathing suit, the one who played the music, and she's running past you, but she stops, and she spreads her arms to shield you from a man, overly pale, who is about to run you down. The extra second gives you a shot and you throw off the crutches. Your arms fling out, awkward, and slap the top of the water as you dive. And I can see again, I can see you're still crying. And it's the saddest I've ever seen you. Or maybe I'm only just seeing it now, how unhappy you are, how badly I've done at making it all okay.

I reach the edge of the pool, and the water is a brilliant white froth, arms and legs. The heavy couple are dousing their toddler in and out of the water, and it's wailing. But you. You're staring up at me from below the surface. Your dark eyes are calm, and for a moment I see that maybe you want it to end. One little slip, a second too late, and it would all be over—the physical torments and that feeling of alienation I recognize on your face when people pretend not to see you, or when they see you all too much.

You sink to the bottom, and I think, this is maybe what you want. Something has made you wise and independent, and there's a wish being communicated. I should hesitate at the edge of the pool a little too long—poor judgment, they'll say. Lost in the hysteria. I should let it go, and by the time the lifeguard gets to you, it'll all be complete. The whole thing. It'll be over. No miracles for us today.

You're still staring. You could swallow the world with that calm.

But you're my son. And I'm sorry. You're my son, and maybe it's selfish, but my shoes are already doing cartwheels as I kick them off. My arms are already two straight lines in front of my face, pointed toward the water. I'm already lunging, feeling the grit of concrete on the bottom of my toe as I leap.

And I'm sorry if my love causes you pain. I'm sorry if surrender isn't my strong suit. But it's got me, too. This life. And it's not something that let's go.

It's got us, son. I'm diving in.

patience is a fruit

First time I saw an angel was a day of gunfire. A whole mess of blackbirds had taken roost in a sandstone cornice above the county courthouse. Squawking like pirates from behind a gunwale, they'd rain shit down on traffic violators, newlyweds, deputies, judges, lawyers, the city auditor, you name it. You spent too much time standing on those broad, concrete steps, you'd take a shot to the eye, a glob down the neck of your collar, or some splatter on your tongue. So it wasn't too much a surprise when Sheriff Keef ordered folks to clear out for blocks so deputies and a few local boys could sharpshoot the fowl with .22s.

Me and Gabe packed our rifles down to Oak Street, grabassing the way men'll do when there's fun to be had, talking big about taking pot shots at the bronze statue of Lady Justice. When we arrived Bill and a few of the other deputies were standing on the sidewalk spitting into the gutter while the sheriff stood in the bed of a truck, meat of his palm hitched on the butt of his pistol.

"Uptown's blocked off and we've moved all the cars.

going anywhere

Remember, boys: clear line of sight. Everyone stays on Main till we give the word. All shots upward. No ricochets. You hear me?"

We nodded. I recognized a few of the faces from the beagle club, a few others from Markham's bar down in the sticks. Fifteen of us, we all marched to the middle of town, the buildings silent except for the birds. People say silent streets are like apocalypse movies, but to me the buildings got all brilliant. The world felt new without people in it, like I could breathe all the sudden.

We spread out in kind of a firing line like an execution squad or an honor guard. Then Sheriff Keef gave the word.

"Raise 'em, boys! Fire!"

Birds burst like party balloons. Steel rounds blistered the courthouse facade, the bullets and buckshot shaving flecks of sandstone from its face. Shiny black corpses plopped into the bushes while sparks ignited loosed feathers in mid-air, turning them into little crescents of flame wafting down among us like Pentecostal blessings. I stopped shooting long enough to follow one burning feather as it danced above the street toward the old feed mill on the other side of the road. The slowness of it imprinted the image on my mind. One single feather. One Jehovah's fire cavorting over these men. Its loveliness tilted to the benevolent wind. Then it dipped into the open hatch of the grain silo.

The explosion of grain dust almost knocked me off my feet. The silo howled, convulsed, and buckled like a beer can. Glenn Flowchet spun with his rifle, scared shitless, squeezed off a round and shot Terry Markham in the face. The bullet shattered Terry's jaw, punched a hole in his cheek, passed out the other side, and whizzed down the street where it bounced with the sound of a dropped nickel.

"Holy shllllit," said Terry. A slurry of blood dribbled out the black hole next to his chin.

"God damn it," Sheriff Keef said. "God fucking damn it."

patience is a fruit

Glenn Flowchet flipped the safety on his gun and set it at his feet, staring at it like it was a dead dog.

Gabe chuckled into his palm—"Holy fuck holy fuck, man. God damn."

Which is when I saw the angel. She was a honey-eyed young woman in pale blue doctor's scrubs. No wings. No harp. Just a mildly plump figure with her hand on Terry's back. She slipped past the others, leading Terry away as the sheriff trailed after. They were at a dead run, headed for the cruiser. And then she was gone. Obscured from view, and vanished. Terry and Sheriff Keef hit the cruiser. Blood blurred its way down the white panel of the passenger door as Keef thrust an old towel at Terry's face.

No one remembered seeing the woman but me. That night at Carla's, after I told her what happened, she kept on about Terry.

"Eileen says he needs two more surgeries, and then he'll have his jaw wired shut for three months."

"Glen feels bad," I said.

"Forget Glen. Glen's small potatoes. There's going to be an investigation. Terry could sue the sheriff's department. The city has money. Maybe the state, you don't know."

I let it drop. I threw out what was really on my mind.

"You ever see an angel?"

"Like a real angel?" Carla's black hair fell to either side of her sharp chin. She searched for an answer in her peas.

"Real angel, I guess."

"You telling me something?" She grinned.

"I might be."

"I guess if you're calling me your angel, you'll want me around for good."

"I'm not saying that."

"But kind of," she went on. "Like a guardian?"

"I don't know."

"That means you'd be stuck with me. For life."

I tightened my lips. I couldn't follow.

"Marriage," she said. "Is that what we're talking about?"

"It's not."

"Well we're going to have it sometime—this conversation. You're forty-three, Jessie, and me not much younger. We're running out of time for babies."

"I was talking about something else," I said.

"Angels," she said. "Like real ones?"

"Forget it."

•　•　•

Two days later, I was back at the foundry. The morning was hot, and Dale had left the bay doors open on the southern side of the mechanics' garage. I was casting clutch covers for motorcycles, pouring steel from a handheld crucible about the size of a lunch pail into sand molds. The steel looked like a liquid sunset and rolled out of the hopper into the forms. Sparks fluttered up as it splashed against the lip and steadied out into tiny glowing lakes above the concrete floor. I'd poured two dozen, all of which sat cooling into mute gray shapes ready for filing down, when my arms started shaking. My muscles weren't what they used to be, even five years ago, but I'd kept strong with building in the summers and working the foundry and splitting logs and picking up shifts weekends at the concrete place, so I was a little worried to find I was tapped out, same as if I'd gone on a drink the night before. Except I hadn't. I'd slept well. Woke up with electric in my veins, is what Gabe would have said. I put down the pot and tried shaking out the muscles in my forearms. I rubbed them down one at a time from the elbow to the wrist.

I picked up the crucible and started to pour when a kid—a boy, maybe five years old in robot pajamas—sprinted in from outside and ducked beneath my handle.

The kid's hand shot out within an inch of the molten steel. I pushed it away from him instinctively, which set me off balance. I felt a muscle pull in my back and dropped the crucible. It made a hard clunk on the floor and tipped. Steel sprawled in a glowing pool across the concrete. It washed up against Dale Everett's boot like waves upon the rocks. Dale swore as he fumbled for his laces. Me and Hanratty jerked Dale back, yanked his pants up to the knee, and hauled him onto the workbench. The liquid steel took three toes before he was out of his sock.

• • •

Nobody else saw no kid, and Gary Souders, the foreman, fired me the next day.

After that I started staying home more, which at first Carla liked. Then she didn't.

"Is this about angels?" she asked a few weeks later. She stood in front of the television.

"No," I said, pointing to the screen. "It's the skins tournament. ESPN."

She didn't find this amusing.

I'd told her about the boy and about seeing him again on top of the Wal-Mart. I'd just stepped out of my car when I saw him up there all alone, on the roof, looking down at the parking lot. All I could do was freeze and gawk up at the kid. My hands trembled as he touched his own temple with a chubby, pale finger. I mirrored the motion, trying to read the meaning in it. A few folks in the parking lot looked up, but none of them stopped, not the way they should have. Not the way you stop when you see a kid on top of a Wal-Mart.

Next day I found out a young woman, an English teacher, died of a brain aneurism by the cart corral that same day. Paper said she was holding her eight-month-old baby when it happened, and the infant didn't make a sound until someone pulled it from her arms. I tried to remember if I'd gone to the store before or after this happened. But I didn't know.

"You seen anymore of these angels?" Carla wanted to know.

"No," I said, though I had. I'd decided they were definitely angels. I'd seen one near the A&P checkout where

89

a six year-old girl fell and cut her knee on some weather stripping. The angel that time was a blonde man in a blue suit who held the automatic door from closing against the girl's fingers as she lay on the mat. There was one, too, in the endzone of the Redmen football game on Friday night. Right there in the goddamn endzone under the arc sodium lights, feet planted in the red grass where the Chief Tecumseh logo had been painted by the field crew. She was a skinny woman with black hair and a bleached out old house-dress the color of dead carnations. She kept looking to the sky and throwing her hands up like her and God were calling for a field goal.

• • •

Sunday I went to church with Gabe. We sat in the third pew from the back with a squat, old man in a flannel shirt and navy Dickies. He wore white gym socks and kept tugging them up his calf, and I kept looking at the liver spots and broken veins in the skin of his legs. His heavy movements made me tired, and I couldn't concentrate properly on the message.

When it came time after the sermon, the pastor asked us if we would accept God into our hearts, and I stood up. Gabe tried to hold me back by hooking his finger into my pocket, but I pulled free and walked to the altar where I kneeled. The pastor was a tall man with curly, dark hair and a thick moustache, his breath the minty tar of menthols, and he leaned over me, put a hand on my head.

"You got sins?" he whispered.

"I do," I said.

"Take them to Jesus. Call his name, and let's pray together."

I thought I'd see an angel then, but I didn't. What I'd meant to do was ask the pastor about them. I wanted to tell him about angels and about not seeing them in my house so that all I wanted to do anymore was hole up in my living room. I wanted to tell him I'd grown up in a church similar

patience is a fruit

to this one, forty or fifty people. Good people I'd known my whole life till I stopped going when I was about eighteen. I tried going back there twenty years later, but all the people had changed, and I was sorry I'd left.

So me and the pastor had a pray, and I didn't see an angel, and I thought about how this might be a new place to start, especially if Carla and me had kids.

Carla met me at the back of the church and asked how I was feeling.

"I feel fine," I said. "I'm good."

"Is this about angels?" She put her pale hand on my forearm.

"It's about family," I said. "Getting right."

Gabe came up with a plump, red-haired woman with a milky face. She walked with a limp, but she also had a good smile.

"This is Shyla," Gabe said. "And this here's her mom."

An even plumper, shorter woman who looked exactly like what Shyla would look like in thirty years, grabbed both my wrists and pulled me toward her. She caught me in a hug and thumped my back between the shoulder blades so my breath came out like slow hiccups.

"Gabe done told us about you losing your job. Figured we might help you."

"Thanks, ma'am, but I don't need charity. Thank you, anyway."

"Ain't charity," she said seriously. "It's work. Honest to God."

Gabe put his arm around Shyla. "Shyla here says her mom needs a couple strong fellas to move some furniture."

"Mom's moving in with me," Shyla said. "Has to haul some things."

I looked at Carla, who was giving me that stare like I was about to evaporate in a blue smoke. She'd been giving me that look for a couple weeks now, and I could feel the lingering tension behind it, the taut band of feelings we had for one another stretching to the snapping point. I was

91

losing her, and as much as I would have liked to stay in my house and wait out the angels, I had to get on, and getting on meant making some money.

"Ma'am," I told Shyla's mom, "I'd be thankful for some honest-to-God work."

She smiled and pulled me in for another hug and another round of back-slapping.

• • •

Next day I got restless. Holing up wasn't doing me a damn bit of good, and if I was going to get on with things I had more than money to consider.

I drove out to Pine Ridge and found the brick house on the hill, no problem. The place wasn't anything fancy; just a one-story structure with a big, old picture window in the front and an above-ground pool off to the side. A thick-haired collie dog who had a few other breeds mixed in came up and sniffed my leg. Then she led me up some stairs from the drive to the front door. Me and her stood there together on the top step as I knocked. A man in his thirties answered. He was skinny and haggard and held a baby that tugged at his earlobes.

"Can I help you?" he said. He looked at the dog with what seemed like disappointment, same way a billionaire might eyeball an inept butler who'd let in the riffraff.

"I'm real sorry to bother you, sir," I said, "but I got something on my mind. And I can't help but think I'm supposed to tell you."

He gently pushed the baby's hands away from his ears. This made the baby laugh.

"Look, bud. I go to church, and this has been a bad week."

"Ain't about church," I said. "Fact is, I just been back there myself, but it's about an angel. I think I seen one on top of the Wal-Mart the day your wife died, and I think maybe it means something."

He blinked and stared at me a good, long while, like you'd

expect. I figured he'd tell me to go to hell, and that'd be that.

Instead, his shoulders slumped. All the grief he'd been holding up loosed itself, and his face sagged.

"Come in," he said.

The dog left me then to attend to her own business, and I followed the man into his living room where he set the baby down in a playpen.

"Name's Allan," he said.

"Jessie," I said.

I told him about seeing the angel—the boy—on top of the Wal-Mart, and how I didn't know whether or not it happened before or after his wife died.

"That was before," he said. "She died late afternoon." He looked like he might cry, but instead he started gathering up baby toys from around the room. When his emotion had passed, he sat back down.

"I guess," I said, "I should apologize. I been seeing angels a while now, and I never know what to think."

He listened to me like I wasn't crazy, and this gave me a bit of bravery to state my mind.

"Thing is I suppose I see 'em for a reason, and maybe I could have saved your wife if I'd have been listening better."

He shook his head. His face looked gray.

"Not unless you were a doctor and you had a CT machine," he said. "Aneurysm. They call them silent killers."

"What do you suppose it means, then?"

I felt like a heel asking this fella for answers when he was probably asking God for plenty himself.

He eyed the baby to make sure it wasn't going anywhere, then motioned I should follow him into the kitchen. He opened the refrigerator for me. It looked to be about a half-dozen casserole dishes chilling under foil.

"See there. Leftovers from where people keep dropping them off. Bud, I don't know what anything means anymore. This food here—it tastes like ashes. Maybe these angels mean something. If they do, maybe that's a good thing. I don't know. Might mean that little boy was Annie's guardian angel." He nodded toward the living room, and I guessed the baby was Annie.

"Keeping her safe," he said. "One thing I know, God works in mysterious ways. That's what they say. And the Bible says patience is a virtue. It's one of the fruits of the spirit."

"I forgot that one," I said.

"Maybe you just have to wait. Find out on God's time."

I drove away from there thinking maybe that Allan just needed someone to talk to, but also thinking the same thing about myself. He'd given me grist for the mill, so to speak.

• • •

Early Saturday we drove to Biddy's house in Gabe's Impala. Biddy is what she told us to call her. Her real name was Jo Beth, and she'd been living alone for eighteen years since her husband took a tumble off the roof of a pole barn in the summer of '94. The Impala was a '74 two-door with a stripe of rust as even as a horizon-line running the middle from headlights to fender. It made a hissy sloughing sound as we rolled over potholes, like the engine was trying to slide out of the chassis.

"You seen the place?" I asked Gabe.

He'd been quiet all morning. He worked a wad of snuff down into his bottom lip and spit into a Sprite bottle he kept wedged between his legs.

"Hey," I said. "You turning into a zombie or something?"

He pulled off the road into a gravel depression that divided the asphalt from a scrubby-looking cornfield. He jammed the car into park.

"Well," I said, "what the hell is it?"

"You got to back me on this, Jessie, you hear?"

"Back you on what?"

"Hear me out. Me and Shyla been talking marriage."

94

patience is a fruit

"Congratulations."

"Shut up. Now her mom is moving in. You see what I mean? I got my place, and Shyla has hers, but we was thinking about consolidating. Move in together. She's got the one girl, Eileen, but I'm ready. I'm ready for that family life, Jessie."

"I hear you," I said. "That's great."

I wanted to tell him about me and Carla, about praying and deciding to go to church from now on, so long as I could get rid of the angels.

"But now that old woman is going to screw things up."

"You talk to Shyla about this?"

"Fought about it, sure. But she says family is family, and I ain't family yet, so I don't have much say."

"You going to convince Biddy not to move in?"

"That ain't going to happen."

"What then?"

"Shyla says her mom has some uppity shit stashed all over the house. Pricey stuff. You help me find some of it, maybe we sell it. We set aside the money for a little apartment for Biddy, something nearby, but out of our hair—somewhere it keeps Shyla happy, and me happy, too."

"Why not make Biddy pay for it?"

"Shyla won't go for it. Her mom walks all over her. But if I pay, she'll listen. It's *for* her anyway, so it ain't like we're stealing."

"She won't notice half her stuff is gone?"

"We're putting it in a storage unit. Give me a week, I'll break the lock and tell her somebody stole it. But I got to take it now, before she moves in and latches on like a tick."

Gabe pulled the car back onto the road without waiting for an answer. I tried to think, so I stared out the window. That's when I saw a man in the cornfield about forty yards out. He wore a black bathrobe and held a plate of eggs in his right hand. His left arm was missing, and a limbless sleeve had been tucked into the fat, front pocket of his robe. I only saw him for a second, but the image left a bitter, twisted

feeling in my gut, like the angels were trying to send me a
message that I was too stupid to understand.

We drove for a while more.

"How long you been thinking about this?"

"About what?"

"About stealing from this old woman? What do you
think?"

"My back's against a wall, Jessie. I ain't never mean to
hurt family, you know that."

"You need my answer?"

"Figured you'd give it to me."

I thought of stealing from the old woman who'd hugged
me in church. I thought of selling Jessie out and ruining a
chance at his new family. Most of all I thought of them angels walking around and if they had a god damn meaning
or if they couldn't care less.

"Carla and me aren't so good. I got to have some money
coming in. Maybe for a ring."

A smile eked across Gabe's lips.

"You stick with me. You'll get yours, square."

●   ●   ●

It was an old farm house, blank as forgetting. The panes
were warped, and the slivered skin of paint trembled under a warm drizzle. We hustled up the steps. Gabe smacked
his hands together and knocked on the door.

Biddy opened it and hugged us. "Just doing my dishes,"
she said, and waved us in.

Our feet made the old floorboards moan. Gabe mapped
the place, ticking off the steps from room to room. I could
see his lips moving. He was taking inventory. In the sitting room there was a small, spotty-looking television with
milky glass like a bubble of smoke. In one corner sat a dusty
stack of John Wayne DVDs. Biddy led us into the kitchen.
In there were splintered cupboards. On the counter was
an iron corn sheller that looked like a medieval surgeon's
tool, and a few horseshoe nails in a red, McDonald's fry

box. Beside a dirty microwave was a row of old ceramic crockery and a lot of other shabby things.

Gabe nodded at some boxes stacked brown against the back wall.

"You do all this packing yourself?"

"I still get around," Biddy said. "Heavy lifting's where they got me."

"You won't need to lift a finger."

"Got new milk, you want it."

"From the cow?" Gabe said.

"Sure enough. Still milkin' 'em till the livestock boys get here on Saturday."

"Eggs, too?"

"I'll fry 'em up. You boys take the upstairs. There's a bureau in the room to the right."

We climbed the steps.

Gabe headed for a door at the end of the hall and motioned for me to explore the room on the left. I heard the skillet and smelled bacon from the kitchen below.

It's been my experience old folks keep all kinds of things, regardless of the inconvenience or the utility. Had a grandmother once kept the box to her bowling ball—the ball was long gone in a church raffle after a broken hip threw a hitch into her release. She kept that box, though, even though she left it empty at the foot of a bed she didn't use. Biddy's place seemed a lot like that. Junk in all the upstairs rooms. Five unopened toaster ovens stacked on top of one another. A George Foreman grill on top of those. Pile of fur coats that when you picked them up shedded heaps of fleecy brown hairs like they had the mange. I poked through some trash bags, and for ten minutes all I found was yarn and more yarn, all of it a dead green color as ugly as a lie. Best thing I could find was a heavy bedside lamp made of lead crystal, and I was holding it when Gabe leaned in to the room and clucked his tongue.

"Jackpot," he said.

He waved me across the hall, and I followed him into

what must have been Biddy's bedroom. On the bureau were some things like a comb and hairpicks. The bed was made, and despite the rain a brittle light played on the windows.

Gabe dropped to one knee by the bed and shoved a hand between the mattress and box spring.

"Oldest goddamn trick in the book," he said, and up-ended the mattress. Wads of cash lay in clumps across the top of the box spring. Most of the bills I could see had Poor Richard himself staring up at us with what to me looked like a grin.

"What are you doing?"

"Grabbing mine," Gabe said. He shoved two piles of cash into his pockets straight away and paused like he was trying to decide if another pile was too much. He turned to me.

"Get on with it."

"I can't."

"You better."

Too late I heard Biddy traipsing up the hall behind me. She shoved me aside and gawked down at Gabe on his knees.

"You better be praying, son," she hissed. Then she ran for the stairs and started squawking out "Help! Help!" and throwing up her arms.

Gabe was after her like a dog. Pushed past me and grabbed at her shoulders. But she was a stout little ox and heaved away from him with all the weight of her upper body, which was considerable. Gabe lost his grip, and she flailed forward. Her arms wheeled and she overshot the top step. I watched her fly out of sight and the sound of the tumble reminded me of an engine dying on a snowy morning, the way the pistons sputter and the block jitters into silence.

Gabe ran to the stairs and looked down.

"Damn," he said. A jackrabbity wildness was in him, and he was breathing heavy. "Damn, Jessie. She's still alive."

A part of me wanted to thank the good lord, but the way Gabe said it I could see this was a worse situation than before.

patience is a fruit

He was looking around now, back in the bedroom, for
something to kill her with. He must have decided it could
wait another few seconds, because he stopped to shove two
more wads into the back pockets of his jeans. He was bent
down over the bed, and I could feel the weight of the lamp
I'd been holding. It was still in my hand. A heavy, burden-
some thing. God said we all have a lamp in us. We carry it
around. And I always took that to be a metaphor for the
soul. A burning for salvation, I suppose. But my lamp had
a weight big enough to crush a man's skull.

Now I heard the moans floating up the stairs. They
sounded the way the widower Allan Robbins did as I left
his house four days before. We'd said our goodbyes, and
he'd shut the door, and halfway down the steps I'd felt reluctant to go. I'd meant to ask him one more thing about
God, so I'd turned around, climbed the steps, and stood
ready to knock when I heard him. From behind the door
he was wailing like a child. His sobs were snagged by gulps
for air. Right there I froze, and I felt a connection with the
man. I thought right then that God is nothing but loss,
and that made us brothers. I knew I should knock. I should
return some of the comfort he'd afforded me. But instead,
I walked away. I was a coward. I gave the collie dog a good
scratch behind the ears and decided never to bother Allan
Robbins again.

Biddy's old voice sounded like Allan Robbins'. It tick-
led the hallway and Gabe grabbed another pile of money.
You had to have patience for God's plan. Patience is what
Allan Robbins told me. A fruit of the spirit. And all the angels had come together because they'd seen this moment
coming. I needed the strength to do what had to be done.
Maybe I couldn't save Tina Robbins, but I could save the
others. I could save Biddy, maybe.

"Fruit of the spirit," I said. I felt a righteous swell working like a light through the darkness of my heart. My lips
tasted sweet as honeysuckle.

I looked down on Gabe and breathed the smell of the

going anywhere

house into my lungs. I could hear the death of everything. I raised the lamp over my head, and its weight felt like the weight of all things. I paused. I could see through the windows that the rain had let up.

They were coming. Across the fields. From the woods. They were coming.

a different-sized us

She emerged from the car and rounded the old house to look across the yard, the ground rampant with weeds. Beyond it a swath of brilliant green cut a kind of fairy path through the woods, and near the trailhead lay an ancient plow and a skeletal tractor, their paint faded to a sun-sapped rose that still clung to the iron of the wheel wells. Patrick made a sound from inside the house as if trying to draw her attention. He'd been moody most of the afternoon, flipping unwanted French fries out of the car as they drove, until he'd eaten so little he begged her to stop again, then got picky with a chicken sandwich and fell asleep. In Patrick's defense, the trip had been unexpected. She hadn't intended to take him from Dale's driveway. That much had just happened. But in her own defense, her actions were planless as osmosis, a current of biological imperatives sliding beneath her and buoying her weight: a mother needs her son.

She turned back to the house. Most of the windows had been broken. Transparent shards jutted in colorless shapes from the panes. Through one—the kitchen, she thought—she could make out Patrick's silhouette swinging something so it thumped the wall. She considered yelling but stopped herself, unwilling to break the cool silence of wind in the elder trees, the rasping quiet of shadows stretching beyond the woods as if to caress the siding.

She took the back stairs, clinging to the old railing and stepping over the holes where the boards had rotted through. Memories of hiding beneath this back porch swirled up unbidden, and she remembered Holly Demerrich, dead now, a girl with freckles and bleached-out eyes pale as untouched bluebells.

She found Patrick inside with a rusty hammer banging away at a loose rung of the balustrade, trying to knock it free.

"What are you doing?"

"I saw a rat in the wall in the kitchen," he said. "The hammer's too short."

Patrick was ten, she thought. Nine or ten. Yet it never ceased to confound her that he should talk so logically, think so much like his father that she sometimes heard Dale's clipped, impatient tones carrying through into her own son's vocal cords and movements. Patrick wasted little energy and possessed it in abundance.

"We're going to fix this place up," she said. "Please don't go tearing it down."

He looked at her, his tender eyebrows knotted darkly over his eyes. "We aren't staying here, are we?"

"I'll get the water turned on. We'll fix the windows."

"How? You don't have any money."

Always the tactician. This was Dale, his rigid temperament coalescing in Patrick's tiny frame. She imagined Dale, rebuilding himself like a robot, over and over again, for countless generations. Copy upon copy, and for a moment she couldn't bring herself to meet Patrick's gaze.

"I have some money," she said.

"Show me it."

"It's in a bank."

He finished knocking out the spindle from the banister. It made a clunk on the dirty floor where she saw vandals had spray-painted vulgarity and indecipherable tags.

"I'm sorry I didn't have time to get things ready," she said.

"I'm hungry."

She lifted her hands slightly. All she wanted to do was to hold him. To have him melt into her. If they'd been able to do such a thing, they may not be here, in her father's old home. It was the one thing she'd never sold, not through any strength of her own, but because the house had been secluded and worthless. No one wanted it. She'd not been here in fifteen years at least, and it felt like exactly that long.

•   •   •

As night stretched itself across the treetops they bedded down in her old Subaru wagon; she reclined in the front passenger seat while he scrunched himself uncomfortably onto the second-row bench. Their things piled high in the back blocked the headlights of occasional cars rolling round the curve of road that connected to the bottom of the drive. But the moan of semis as they engine-braked down the hill always woke her in time to see those lights casting thicketed shadows across the face of her old house. Twice she thought she saw the figures of men inside and gripped her ivory-handled pocket knife so hard her joints ached. She stared into the residual darkness of the windows awaiting some confirmation of movement, but it never came, or always played as the trick of her eye, and sometimes she was certain they were watching her from inside.

Finally she reached for the backpack at her feet and slipped a baggie out of its side pocket. She didn't want to smoke, so she snorted the heroin, resorting to her store of the costlier stash for safety's sake. The drug flowed into the back of her neck, worked its way up her skull, then dropped all the way into her toes. Before falling asleep, she wondered how the moon ever found its way back to earth.

•   •   •

In the morning she awoke with a layer of dry mucus coating her tongue. She checked herself for vomit, then the back seat. Patrick was gone.

She looked for him in the house before traipsing out to the backyard and calling his name. Slender tribes of dandelions had sprouted up overnight. Their puckered yellow heads bristled against the cold.

"Patrick!"

The fairy path led away and up the hill. She had a vague memory of its curves, its undefined narrowing as it neared the spring from which her father used to fetch drinking water when the well was tainted. She remembered the brackish, rusty taste of the well when the dog fell in and her mother was forced to boil the water before filling their glasses. That was in the winter when the spring had frozen solid. They hadn't gone to school then, not until Child Protective Services threatened to remove her and her brother from the household. The government people had called it that—the household, which put her in mind of a structure with arms and a warm embrace pulling them close and brushing outsiders from its porch with one sweep of its massive, cedar-sided hands.

She followed the path through the woods until it terminated at the spring. Its flow had weakened in the intervening years, but still came nonetheless. Her father had plugged a black, plastic pipe about two inches in diameter into the rock, and the brilliant, clear water poured out of it into a shallow creek bed of rounded pebbles, most the size of marbles and tennis balls. They were uniformly brown and talked like old friends.

Above the creek, a blunt, mossy rock face of pitted granite rose about thirty feet, and a fissure cleaved its way up the center. Above that the woods resumed in their gently sloping ascendancy to the top of the larger hill. She wriggled into the cleft of the cliff and found footing in the roots of trees which, from high above, had sent themselves deep through the stone in search of the water below. Maybe it was they who had split the rock. She didn't know. She began to climb and felt the roots against her palms like the shaking of old hands.

She reached the top and took in the view. The house was obscured by the black birch trees already displaying their new leaves. But the sun had cast its light over a hollow to the right. Here the valley dipped back down into a carpet of white crocuses, their tender petals so close to one another that the dark humus of leaves and earth below appeared only at their edges. It was as if a blot of snow had fallen silently in the woods and sanctified this one small oval of ground. This reminded her of something, and suddenly she wished Patrick could see. He'd understand then the things she was unable to tell him. Her brain felt muddied, and all she could think of relating was about the time when she was twelve, when she finally went to school in town and waited at a Friday-night dance for any boy, any one at all, to ask her onto the floor, and how that had been her only chance, and when no boy asked, she had never gone to another dance in her life.

She regretted it more than anything. More than leaving Patrick and Dale even. She wanted to tell Patrick just that one story about herself, here, in the presence of all those flowers, because then he would have to understand the something she'd always known about beauty that she'd never been able to express. She watched the sun strengthen and the crocuses widen their outstretched arms so that they became indistinct, blurred as an overexposed photograph.

She thought of calling for Patrick from this height, certain her voice would expand to the rest of the world even. But she remained quiet. The quiet held the crocuses. The quiet held her secrets. She couldn't shatter that for Patrick.

Not for anybody. She crawled back down the fissure, clutching again at the knobbed toes of the trees. On the way back along the path she slapped her dirty palms against her jeans and felt the heat of the contact in her thighs and hands. She breathed the vinegar scent of crabapple plants, working their stringent life into her sinuses, and reached the edge of the woods ready to call her son's name.

But the sight of the well stopped her short. The well lay about twenty yards from the house. It's stone lid had been rolled away and now rested against the concrete lip. She tried to remember if she'd noticed this last night. The well, a little bigger than a manhole, was shadowed by the canted lid from the morning light and looked cool and quiet near the crystalline blades of grass exposed to the sun. A different kind of quiet came pouring from that deep, black hole, and its silence touched everything with its slender fingers.

She kept her distance from it and slipped around to the front of the house where she stared at her car. She'd left the door open and wondered at the fact that this could be done out here, with no one around to grab your wallet, no one to steal the phone you left on the dashboard or even the car itself. This felt like a good thing, a place to start.

She touched the hood, its cool skin warming with the day, and called her son's name in long syllables: "Patrick!"

A silence echoed back to her. She climbed into the car and drew a breath, smelled her old things, wrapped in bubble packing and cigarette smoke, turning stale in the back of the Subaru. Then she honked the horn three times.

"Patrick!"

Still he didn't answer. She waited, turning the keychain with its clutch of plastic knicknacks over in her hand so it made the sound of junk rolling down a hill, same as when her father took her and her brother to the ravine to discard an old washer, a pesticide drum, and once a rusted Coke machine. Her father would pull off the old county road where the trees separated into bramble and greenbrier, and he'd heave old appliances from the truck bed, send them toppling end over end to the creek a hundred feet below. The Coke machine had been an antique probably. Her father bought it from Markham's store when it went out of business, and he bragged about haggling it down to just thirty-five dollars. It was the kind that held glass bottles and opened from the top, no taller than waist-high, and he'd claimed he was going to plug it into the wall in the living room so the kids could have Coke whenever they wanted. They'd cheered and laughed hauling it back from Markham's, but the welfare people had come that afternoon, were waiting, in fact, to inspect the home. Her father had shouted from the truck at the government people about having no right to show up unannounced. When the woman responded that it was difficult to call without a phone on this end, her father had leaned out his window and said the only thing his daughter could now distinctly remember about him. "You think you're better than me," he said. "But you're not. No one's better than nobody." He'd commanded the children from the cab, spun out in the drive, and disappeared with the Coke machine still knocking against the tailgate where he'd tied it down. He was arrested that night on a drunk and disorderly, and when he made it home four days later, she and her brother were going to school in town. The Coke machine was deposited carelessly into the yard, where it rusted until they finally drove it to the ravine.

She let the keys fall into the passenger seat and thought about honking again. From somewhere trilled a phone, a high-pitched ping and a muffled rap song to which she couldn't understand any of the words. She dug through Patrick's things and found a cell phone at the bottom of his backpack wrapped in a pair of Levi's. She felt hurt. He'd lied to her about not having one. She hadn't heard it ring yesterday, but he must have turned it on in the night, maybe to call or text. Or play a game; it was one of those. It had gone silent by the time she found it in the left leg of the jeans but immediately jumped to life again in her hands.

She touched the button that said TALK. Dale's voice came across the line.

· "Patrick? Patrick? If your mom is there, just pretend like you're humming a song or something. Okay, buddy?"

"He's not here," she said.

"What the hell do you mean he's not there? For fuck sake, I can't believe you'd do this. I can't believe it."

"You don't need to worry."

"Don't need to worry? Are you kidding me? Are you honestly telling me that? You kidnapped our son, Julia. Our son. I'm on my way, and he'd better be safe and sound. He'd better be goddamn hunky dory."

He said corny things like this when he was angry. Hunk dory.

"We just wanted to spend time together," she said.

"Oh now. Now. You need time. Convenient."

"Did you say you're on your way?"

It came to her. Patrick, growing restless in the night, texting his father to come and get him. And like that it was over. Their time away from the static of human voices and the scuttling concerns of everyday living. She hung up the phone.

She still had time to tell him what she meant to say. She'd find him and tell him and things would be different even after Dale took him back to the world with Sandy and the house on Green Parkway and the automatic ice maker in the door of their refrigerator. The Coke machine and the refrigerator and the keys and the phone all seemed to her at this moment to be the same thing. The same item filled up with whatever human life got poured into them. She wanted to tell Patrick this, because none of them compared to the white crocuses in the woods. But time was cracking apart, falling into holes in the earth as Dale drove and drove.

She took a bump of her good stuff for clarity. One small sniff. Then another. And another. Colors flattened out, then attached themselves to objects again. She left the car and began shouting. She came upon the back yard the way you run into a stranger climbing the stairs from the subway. Like light and form have taken shape simultaneously. Her son stood near the well with a white crocus in his hand. His skin had gone gray. Clear rivulets trickled from his eyes like a little fountain in a southern garden. His clothes were soaked and dark as dish water.

"I'm dead now," he said, and a frog wriggled wetly from between his lips. It leapt from his tongue and landed in the grass. "I'm dead now," he repeated.

The aggregation of trees and house and the junked tractor felt suddenly disorderly, as if they'd spun about in a clothes dryer and tumbled forth.

"Careful now," she said. "Careful. That well is dangerous."

Something had gone wrong; she'd mistaken her stashes, maybe, or taken too much, or maybe this was some fresh malady, a new way for her mind to hollow out the details and turn them to ash the way it always had since she was very young. Her bones felt like jelly. She lowered herself and crawled toward her son on hands and knees. She felt the tiny bits of stone in the earth belied by the long grass. This was hard soil. A planter's nightmare. All her father had been able to grow was a single pumpkin that sprawled out through the wild tangle of bearbind and ironweed and quivering fescue. The wild plants had obscured the pumpkin until one day she sighted it fully formed, its fat orange ribs bulging from the brush. Which was how it felt with Patrick from the very beginning. She didn't remember the pregnancy so much as holding the solid weight of him against her chest and trying to fathom how he'd come about. He was her pumpkin. She'd thought that several times; though she refrained from making it a pet name. The pumpkin was another of her secrets.

She reached the well, but her dead son was gone, and she couldn't remember if she'd witnessed the moment he vanished. Now the lip of the well was in her hands. Its concrete was the same cool irregularity as the roots of the trees.

going anywhere

Something struck her buttocks. She looked up to see Patrick again, though his skin had revived and his clothes, like the house and woods before, had sucked the color back into themselves. He kicked her again.

"Why are you on the ground?"

"I thought you were dead," she mumbled.

He peered over the well, and she instinctively raised her hands to keep him from getting near it.

"You think I'm stupid," he said sullenly. He made a face that turned his lips into a fish's. She couldn't look at his silhouette against the sky. She felt sick. She desperately wanted him to help her up, to hold out his hand and haul her to her feet. If he did this, if he made contact, it would right her. The whole dryer-tumbled world would realign into a pathway with rails and signs and escalators directing her forward. If only he would reach out.

"I don't think you're stupid," she said.

"Then why don't we ever do stuff I want to do? Why do we always have to go to your stupid places?"

"We can go wherever you want."

"That's a lie," he said. "You're lying."

One touch, and she'd be healed like Lazarus, arisen from the grave. Because her son was Jesus. He was a healer. A magic pumpkin.

"You admit it," he said. "You say you're lying or I'm jumping in the well."

"I'm not lying," she said. "I'll take you anywhere. Any place. You name it."

Her voice had begun to slur and her arms filled with what felt like gallons and gallons of warm water. She couldn't lift them. A sadness went swishing around in her blood.

"You're lying." He stepped up onto the well and straddled it, looking into the black eye of the water below.

"Why are you doing this to me?" she said. "Get down from there." Her voice had moved to the left of her, and she worried her words would run away before she could convince him of her sincerity.

110

"I'm jumping," he said. "I'm jumping in the well, and you have to save me unless we go somewhere right now."

Her bones had grafted themselves to the earth's every stone. Her desperate heart pressed against her lungs. She'd never breathe again. If he jumped, if he died. If something happened all because of her silly wish to explain what beauty was, she would follow him. She'd tumble in after, and both of them would be flushed to hell.

"You're Jesus," she said.

"Huh?"

"You're Jesus. You're my Jesus. Don't forsake me."

That word, forsake, she'd learned in the church basement at twelve, and it had followed her all over until it sprang, quivering and angry, to the ground at her son's feet.

He put a finger to his chest. "I'm Jesus?"

"Jesus."

"Bible Jesus?"

"Bible Jesus. You're Jesus. Just don't jump, don't go away, and I'll take you anywhere."

A smile slid up his face. He scratched his stomach. "If I'm Jesus, then you're forgiven," he said. He was mimicking what he'd heard in Sunday school, repeating compact phrases like she had done. "You're healed." He reached down and tapped her forehead, almost pitching forward into the hole. "Because I am Jesus," he said. His arms made wide circles as he restored his equilibrium. "I am Jesus." He turned it into a song. Then he spit into the well.

She heard it slap the water below. She heard it rippling through everything.

And that was all.

• • •

Because there is no end. The moment cannot conclude. An echolalia of greater voices recur, second by second, in the blurring wash of time. The sound of the world becomes a child's babble, a repetition of utterances that have made up its earlier days. She thought this on some level, how the ripples had struck a note in her bones that would vibrate for years. How a single day is a lifetime if it's important.

For twenty-four of those years she held that moment by the well fixed in her mind. The future is ever present, she thought. A pun. The words of a wise man or a slack-shouldered, stand-up comedian.

She didn't see Patrick but four more times. Deputies had arrived. Dale had appeared. She was taken away and survived. Then Patrick began mailing her birthday cards and Christmas greetings after his first year in college. He'd tried to explain to her in a few scrawled lines about a class he'd taken on comparative religion, about why it was important to be forgiven, but she couldn't discern to which one of them he was referring, himself or her. He never asked to meet, and she did him the courtesy of reciprocating with silence. In the following years his cards became more calculated, the handwriting darker and more confident, the lines growing meticulous, and she imagined him gathering up order to his life like a cloak. He always, from the very beginning, signed the cards, *Love, Jesus*. Their private joke.

A week after her sixtieth birthday, Dale called to tell her Patrick had been in a car wreck, the world had grown dim. He's a father of three, and a hell of a human being, Dale said. Dale cursed the drunk who'd skittered through lonely, Sunday streets, cut across parking lots, shaved paint from parked cars, and found their son in a nameless intersection on an errand for morning coffee. Dale's voice had become civil to her somewhere in the index of years.

"He's in surgery," he said. "It's 'touch and go.' That's what the doctor said. Those are the words he used."

She said okay. Okay. It was all she could think to utter. After she hung up she wished she'd thanked him for calling. He wasn't obligated.

She drove out to the old house, which had bided its time, acquiring a slump from its rotting foundation. The two of them, she and the house, had become gray, succumbing to the disrepairs of age somewhat. A pair, she thought. She had meant to give the land to Patrick, to sell it or do with whatever he pleased. She had hoped if she did this that, as an adult, he would wander the woods and find the crocuses, that he would understand why she had brought him out here as a child. But the truth was she hadn't trusted the message to cross the gap, did not have faith in her own capability to project her meaning over the dividing line of communication. The beauty had remained her secret.

The crocus blooms were out of season, and she entered the hospital without one. He was out of surgery, the wife told her. The wife, who was civil, whose eyes were puffy, and whose children orbited her and bumped against her legs like chicks. They were all still small, still young, younger, than Patrick had been on the day they had spent together.

She looked in on her son. She hadn't set eyes on him in years. Not since the last hearing. The left side of his face had developed a purple bloat like a tumorous potato. His hand lay in a cast at his side. Dale rose from a seat near the window and hugged her, and Sandy did the same. They sat back down and watched her. She stood at the foot of her son's bed and gently touched his toe.

Here he was again, wholly formed anew. A new pumpkin. A new Jesus, with his new beauty. His new family. Wholly formed, the way all things in life were revealed to her.

They were still small, she thought again. The children. Life was still in its bloom. There was still time.

"Wake up, Jesus," she whispered. "Wake up, and I'll tell you everything."

butterscotch

From where he stood in his kitchen, Arthur could see the long line of hostas separating the woods from the close-cropped perennial ryegrass of his back lawn. The hostas had been planted by Alexis at the beginning of spring and interspersed with brilliant yellow tulips, which she had buried in the early winter according to USDA recommendations for climate-hardiness zone six. Alexis was a planner. Arthur liked that about her, and the hostas and tulips attested to the rightness of their lives together. They'd been married only two years. They were what her mother called "career-blind," wed too late, but they were not lacking for money and therefore comfort. They were happy.

The only liability was the question of children. The matter of childbearing, child-rearing, had come up lately. The problem had emerged fully formed as an increasingly pressurized point like a swelling bruise. Doubts about whether or not it was too late seemed to flit back and forth between them. One day Arthur would be certain he could hack it. He was only thirty-seven. Fifty-five or -six when the child graduated high school. Alexis would be a breezy fifty-three. But the next day, despite a weeklong diatribe about prenatal health, violin lessons, tuition, and whatever else, Alexis would be the one to turn suddenly upbeat. She'd emote a relaxed and ready demeanor, and on those days, without fail, Arthur would recant his own earlier impetuosity, claiming he preferred the comfortable amenities of the childless, the relaxed retirement years, jetting off, unencumbered by family, to one day wander the Hierapolis ruins—just him and Alexis—and walk the windy shoreline of the Aegean.

Then, only yesterday she'd finished their debate by showing him the pink plus sign on the "pee-stick." She handed it to him across the breakfast table, and all he could think to say was, "Should we be holding that over the bacon?"

They didn't talk much after that, not yesterday, and now, in the early morning of a lazy Saturday, he'd let her sleep in, preferring the time to process alone, to sip coffee and look at the lawn, the hostas, the tulips.

After a short while, the world felt still again. He breathed in, out, in.

And something emerged from the woods.

•   •   •

Zombies or ghosts. These were prevalent theories in the early days. Though they didn't attack, didn't show signs of being angry or malevolent. And they had substance, could be felt and prodded. Which ruled out both explanations. Not zombies. Not ghosts. But something else.

The first sightings occurred in New York, which gave rise to the idea they were victims of 9/11, resurrected. They appeared to be made of the dust from vacuum bags, looked like people for the most part, though their faces were haggard, old without being aged. And their skin was a mottled pigeon color, the unfinished gray of industrial cabinets. Their clothes were rags, versions of what they may have worn in life, though not all such clothing could be attributed to certain time periods, and upon inspection this attire seemed to be a part of their tired flesh.

Someone called them "travelers," and the name stuck. They moved continuously. Walked or shuffled. They ambled like lost souls and left slight traces of ash, the way a burning cigarette dragged along the asphalt might.

Authorities made attempts to capture them. If stopped, the travelers disintegrated into a pile of feathery ash that could not be collected, but instead blew away on the wind. More intricate methods were developed, roving collection containers with treadmill bottoms, which swept the travelers up into what looked like large glass tubes and kept them walking. But within seconds the captured would fall apart and be ground into the rolling belt, then disappear entirely.

Despite this, people had touched them and confirmed their corporeal existence. Churches sprang up along what were dubbed "migration routes," paths known to be heavily traversed by travelers. For weeks, parishioners prayed in newly erected sanctuaries that still smelled of sawdust, rushing out when the bell rang to touch them, to beg them for answers about the afterlife, for news of loved ones.

The travelers never spoke.

•   •   •

Arthur shook Alexis out of her sleep and pulled her into a sitting position.

"Artie, stop it," she whined. "I'm not a rag doll."

"It's a traveler," he said, and her eyes cleared. She wobbled to the closet and pulled on a robe and followed him to the kitchen. They stared out the wide bay window at the figure shuffling across their lawn. Its feet made tracks in the dew-heavy blades.

"I've never seen one up close," she said. "Only on the news."

"It's not that uncommon," he said. "Statistics say one in five people have direct contact."

They watched the traveler a while. It was male, if these things had genders. That was another debate. He was five-nine or maybe a little more, and thin but with a slight paunch. The crinkled stems that formed his legs moved like a marionette's, herky-jerky with a hitch that, only every few seconds, seemed to defy gravity.

Alexis retreated to the counter for a cup of coffee.

"Should you be drinking that?" Arthur said.

"It's fine. I'm allowed a little caffeine." She sipped it slowly.

They watched the traveler for nearly an hour until he finally crossed the grass and disappeared again into the woods on the other side of the lawn.

"Well, that was interesting," she said.

"I still wonder what they are."

"You and just about everybody else on the planet." She set her empty mug in the sink.

• • •

The arrival of the traveler, the jolt, the newness of it, had broken their stalemate. When he climbed into the shower with her, she didn't shrug him off. He wrapped his arms around her from behind and felt the very hot water sluicing down her neck and against his chest.

They were together in their decisions after that. They agreed on a stroller and a diaper bag. In anticipation of the baby shower, they registered for necessary items at department stores, and Arthur didn't just acquiesce to her desires. He gave input. He made comments about the color of the walls in the nursery. They laughed in Babies "R" Us at their own ignorance about breast pumps.

A few weeks later, the traveler returned. He crossed their yard once in the morning and going the other way at dusk. Arthur watched him. The next day, too. It became a routine—crossing from right to left (north to south) in the morning, left to right at dusk. Equally routine was Arthur in his kitchen at those hours, staring and speculating.

"Where do you go?" he said aloud, and sometimes, as evening drew heavy over the yard and Alexis napped upstairs, Arthur felt a kinship with this wandering thing, as if the two of them were sharing the silence and the ongoing movement of being.

* * *

Toward the end of her first trimester, Alexis grew very ill. Their OB/GYN discussed low progesterone levels.

"Nothing to worry about," she said. "I'll write a prescription for an oral, and I'll check you in a week or so. We'll keep an eye on it."

Alexis smoothed her blue hospital gown. From his hard plastic chair next to the examining table, Arthur raised his hand.

"Yes?"

"Could there be other factors at work?" he said. "Something environmental?"

"Do you have something in mind?"

"Travelers," he said, and looked at the floor. "There's been one in our yard. For nearly ten weeks. Since we've known about the pregnancy, actually."

The doctor, who was short and a little chunky, with an out-of-date haircut, who for all these reasons came off as guileless, tapped the examination table with Alexis's file. "We can't know that," she said, then hesitated.

Alexis, swinging her legs nervously, stopped. "Have you heard something?"

"Not per se," the doctor said. "But I can't lie. There seems to be . . . a correlation."

"With pregnancies?" Arthur said. "Illness? Miscarriage? What?"

At "miscarriage," Alexis flinched.

"I did not give this to you," the doctor said. She peeled off a sticky-note from a large pad and wrote down the name of a website.

* * *

TheTruthAboutTravelers.com said the baby needed love, that a lingering traveler, which it defined as any such entity remaining within a five-mile radius or seen frequently (within a period of days) recrossing the same land, was a sign of doubt.

Doubt.

"About the baby?" Arthur said. It was late. He and Alexis were in bed, and Alexis had her computer open on her lap.

"Why?" she said. "Do you have doubts about the baby?"

The morning she had told him she was pregnant, he'd hinted to her that he might be fine with an abortion. He hadn't said this in so many words, but knew they were both in agreement—it *was* an option. She had shut down the discussion. No. She did not have doubts. "You'd better get on board with this," she'd said.

Now, in bed, staring at the website, he said, "I don't have doubts. None. It can't be that."

He lifted her hand off the keyboard and squeezed it lightly.

●　●　●

Alexis's mother arrived on Tuesday with two hard purple suitcases. She smelled like a mixture of stew and lingering aerosols. Built like a toy train, squat and bulky, Mama Junie drew Alexis in with one arm and hooked Arthur around the waist with the other.

"How's my grandbaby?" she said.

She looked down at Alexis's stomach, still flat, obscured beneath a loose plaid shirt.

"It's a boy," she said. "I can tell by the way you're carrying it."

That night Arthur experienced the momentary solace of sharing his worry for Alexis. Together he and Mama Junie doted, they rested hands on Alexis's shoulders, they prepared desserts, they did dishes, discussed hospital routes and mobiles. In the sudden release, Arthur imbibed of three after-dinner brandies and brought up the topic himself of Mama Junie staying on for the long haul.

So it was very much his own mistake. He would think this later. Very much.

going anywhere

• • •

She remade the house in her own image. Days when Alexis and Arthur were away at work, which was most of them, Mama mounted a comprehensive assault on the interior that would have impressed the most strategically minded generals of history. The appearance of sickly-sweet butterscotch-scented candles began with an innocent votive-sized one on the sideboard in the hallway. When Arthur first expressed his distaste for the scent, Alexis chided him: "It's one candle. It's nothing. Besides, I kind of like it. It's like candy. It fits."

"What fits?" he'd said.

"I don't know. For the baby. Butterscotch is sweet. So is our little boy."

"So you think it's a boy now?"

Within a week, the candles were everywhere, big fat ones on the kitchen countertop, medium-sized ones on the backs of all the toilets, even in the master bathroom, so the whole house smelled like a confectioner's, a scent that blasted Arthur in the face when he arrived home.

There were also new throw pillows and strangely shaped wooden utensils in an alien crock near the sink, not to mention the parade of drugstore accoutrements for Alexis's aches, for her sudden and unaccustomed lethargy—the footbaths, humidifiers, warming gels, cooling gels, homeopathic teas, and a whole new set of towels and washcloths for upstairs and down, all, of course, the color of butterscotch.

Mama Junie didn't stop there. She began an equally well-orchestrated propaganda campaign. Every time Alexis groaned, at every sibilant intake of breath, Mama Junie shot an obvious glance of reproof Arthur's way. She dropped hints about his shirked duties, his questionable competence in a crisis.

"Remember," she said, "at the reunion—that poor child on the slide?"

"It was minor," Alexis said. They were eating lo mein Arthur had picked up on the way home. He'd promised to cook, then worked late, and resorted to takeout. It had sent Mama Junie on a tirade about MSG and unborn babies that lasted so long he was almost glad she'd moved on to the reunion story, which was one of her favorites in the rotation.

"The child," she said, "got halfway down the slide and decided to jump off."

"We know what happened, Mama," Alexis said. She was a peacemaker, Alexis.

But Junie went on: "Hurts his poor little ankle, and what does Arthur do? Just stands there, staring."

"I was asking him where it hurt," Arthur said limply.

"Troy came to the rescue, thank God. Otherwise that poor soul would probably still be on the ground crying."

"It was a year ago," Arthur said, "and Troy pulled off the kid's shoe and sock before the kid could tell him it was the wrong foot."

"I'm just saying. You have children, you have crises. It's two-plus-two-is-four. And I have to wonder, I just have to— you can't stand over a baby and ask it why it's bawling."

In bed that night, Alexis rolled toward him and said, "You sure you're ready?"

He pretended to be sleeping.

• • •

Another two months went by, and Alexis felt worse still. Through a combination of amassed sick leave and tasks that could be done remotely, this once unstoppable, unflappable, incomparable, pre-dawn-runner, queen-of-the-thirteen-hour-workday started doing business from home all but one day a week. Most of her afternoons were now spent on the couch, laptop plopped on a pillow, her face gaunt as a corpse's, while her mother bustled from room to room. Practically the only time they left the house was when Mama Junie sporadically whisked Alexis and "Joshua" off to a new doctor's appointment, a new round of blood tests.

Arthur asked Alexis why her mother had suddenly named the child. "We still don't know the sex," he said.

Looking drained and defeated, Alexis stared up at him. "I don't know. I guess it's okay. I kind of like it." She picked at the quilt on her lap, and he didn't have the heart to take it further.

• • •

Arthur began spending his evenings on the patio. The interior smells, the sudden nest-like quality of his overly warm home, the drawn look of his wife, her skin ashen, her silence, was all too much after a full day. It was late summer, and he added a second iced whiskey to what had once been a strictly one-drink, three-nights-per-week ritual. These evenings, as Mama Junie puttered about the house, cooking, crocheting, the television playing *Jeopardy*, *Wheel of Fortune*, crime show after overly gory crime show, irate talking heads, and endless sitcoms, Arthur shut the thick glass door behind him, took a seat, and watched the blurring red sun backdrop the trees. The grass each night would turn blue and lose color as twilight set in.

Then, inevitably, around the bottom of the first glass, would come the traveler. Arthur watched him, sometimes toasted him silently, sometimes simply let him go. Other times his stomach knotted, and he would swear the thing had looked his way.

One evening the traveler was late. Mama Junie had dragged Alexis off to the drugstore for a long list of vitamins and supplements to which she'd been adding for the past week, items like fish oil, biotin, and whatever else she wrote on a newly implemented magnetic board on the refrigerator.

The house was especially dark and quiet behind Arthur now. He listened. Shadows had begun to fill all the open spaces, and he could barely make out the tree line when the traveler finally stepped onto the lawn.

Something about tonight, about this time—maybe the

third whiskey on which he'd just begun—made Arthur rise when he saw it. Stepping from the porch, he kicked off his shoes and felt the grass lacing up through his toes. He walked to the traveler's side and stared. In the dark its features looked more human. Put anything in the right light, Arthur thought, and your brain tries to make sense of it. The strange skin, the odd way its body fit together—these details, when dipped in the late-night gloom, became the edge of a lapel, perhaps, the crease of a pants leg, a collar, a watch.

Standing near it, as close as he would to another man at a garden party, Arthur took a drink and spoke. "What are you doing here, bub?"

No response.

He listened to the tired sloughing of its feet through the grass.

"If this is about us, about the baby, you're barking up the wrong tree. I've got no doubts."

Still no reply.

He suddenly hated this figure dragging ass across his lawn. The problem was this: in denying his doubt, Arthur had admitted it. The traveler reminded him of this fact.

That wasn't it, though, not entirely, not unequivocally. The problem was how to express that fine dust of inexpression, the lingering worry that, should he confess to it, would incriminate him. His doubts were half-formed inklings only, a fog of foreboding formed by a million particulates of indecision, vacillation, anxiety. How to communicate to his son what it meant to be a good man? How to express that boundless joy he'd feel when he was in love? How to console a child so mucked and deep into pubescent angst that suicide becomes a hot-glowing option as reasonable as fixing a tuna sandwich or choosing a television channel? How how how? How to express to Alexis that it was not doubt about having a child, but about everything else, about cracking open some new world and just walking around in there, all the while pretending to be the tour guide in a jungle about which you didn't have the slightest knowledge, not about the flora or fauna or the pitfalls?

And wasn't that it? Because if we'd mastered all this talk, all this passing-on from one generation to the next, why weren't we the more stable for it? No, Arthur's fear was not about raising a child, it was about whether or not you could ever communicate anything to anyone, especially the person who needed it most. His inability to convey this to Alexis only solidified the fact that real contact might very well be impossible.

"What's your name?" he said.

Again no answer from the traveler.

Arthur reached out. He felt suddenly angry. He wanted to give the thing a shove, give it a hard poke in the shoulder the way people did if they wanted to start a fight. At the last second he held back. For all the reasons a traveler could not be caught, this one felt precious. Arthur didn't want to see it go. He'd become accustomed to its company.

"Fine. I'll give you a name. How about Joshua? How's that?"

In his slightly befogged mind, the name didn't register until a second after it crossed his lips. He'd said the first name that came to him, the first one at hand, the one he heard a hundred times a day from Mama Junie—Joshua this and Joshua that.

But once it was out, he couldn't change it. It was as if the traveler suddenly had an identity, irrevocable: Joshua, same as a tree was a tree, a rock a rock, a cloud a mutable wisp of white nothing.

Arthur turned away and headed back toward the house. "Good night, Joshua. If you decide to speak, you know where to find me."

•   •   •

The next month Alexis took a turn. She vomited most of the night and found spotting in the morning. The three of them raced to the hospital on still-deserted dawn roads.

butterscotch

Mama Junie muttered prayers in the backseat with Alexis; Arthur came to rolling stops at all the intersections.

A technician performed the ultrasound, and the spotting was written off as minor, related perhaps to Alexis's illness, which was credited to bad tandoori chicken. Mama Junie took it as another opportunity to rail against MSG.

Despite reassurances, Alexis was held for a few hours of observation. While she rested, Arthur walked out to the parking lot and made a phone call to the people at TruthAboutTravelers on their 800 line. Further mysteries could be revealed for a price. He had to pony up for the prime info. There were what the woman called "distribution centers" in nearly every city where the "literature" could be obtained. She gave him the address nearest him and wished him a "blessed night."

He hung up and looked out across the highway running past the hospital. From a scrubby tract of land where a house had been torn down a traveler was approaching the road. This one looked female. She swung her arms in slow, long parabolas, giving her an apish quality. She reached the berm and took one step out into the oncoming lane. A car swerved and managed to miss her by a hairsbreadth, but a pickup close behind sideswiped her and spun her around. As she fell away toward the ditch, she came apart. Her limbs cracked and bits of her fluttered up like a million gray butterflies. Then the rest of her was gone, slumped into a pile and blown away.

The truck never stopped.

• • •

In a strip mall off 270 was a small shop with an orange sign that read *Water Beds and Other Fine Furnishings*. Stepping inside was like returning to the scene of a fashion crime. Blisteringly bright magenta sheets adorned a row of beds with cheap headboards. A hodgepodge of velveteen recliners, particle-board end tables, and lava lamps were arranged on display in what looked like an approximation of a stoner's living room. In the back was a glass counter with a cash register, and behind it were rows of samurai swords in all colors.

Arthur approached the bleach-blonde man sitting there on a stool.

In the display case between them were knives with no conceivable function—blades with brass knuckles built into the handle, points that turned back in a sudden S shape. Others were adorned with so many pewter dragons they looked impossible to hold.

The clerk, middle-aged, was the unhealthy color of a man who's been drinking too long in Key West.

"I'm here about the truth," Arthur said.

"The truth?"

Arthur lowered his voice. The possibility he was falling prey to a scam had left him reticent and ashamed. "The truth. About travelers."

"Oh, that," the man said. He pulled a booklet from a cardboard box on the floor. The "literature" was thin, not more than twenty-five sheets of copy paper stapled in the center and folded over with a stiff paper cover.

"Fifty-nine dollars," the man said.

Arthur gave him sixty in cash and left without change.

• • •

He arrived home to hear Alexis weeping upstairs. Mama Junie met him at the door.

"What's wrong?" he said.

"She's convinced she's never getting better. She can't keep any food down. I called the doctor, and he said if we bring her in, they're probably going to put her on an IV. She absolutely refuses."

He pushed past her and found Alexis in bed, turned away from him.

"Hey," he said. "Is there anything I can do?"

"We ruined everything," she said. "We brought that thing into our lives, and now our baby is going to die."

126

"The traveler? Is that what you mean?"

"Of course that's what I mean. Lauren Kutner said when they were thinking about having a baby, they'd been arguing a whole lot over it. They didn't know if they even wanted kids, and then that thing showed up. They kept seeing it near the cul-de-sac, and her husband—remember Mike?—he hit the traveler with a crowbar. And the next day when she went to the doctor she found out she couldn't have kids." The crying overtook her.

"I'm not following this logic," he said. "Do you want me to get rid of it?"

"Weren't you listening? You can't. Don't you touch it."

"Ally, this is a medical thing. We have to sort it out. We'll take you to the hospital. They'll help."

She sat up and turned on him. Her face was a deep red. "Don't you get it, Artie? It's us. It's not medical. There's all this junk in the world, all this psychic junk, and it's finally caught up with us."

"I don't see how we fit into this. Is this more Lauren Kutner stuff?"

"It's not anybody's stuff. It's true," she said. "Artie, I don't want to go to the hospital because the longer we waste time, the longer we're in danger. Me and Joshua."

"So what are you saying we should do?"

"It's you, Artie," she said. "You're the one."

"The one what?"

"I don't have doubts," she said. "Mama doesn't have doubts. Not about Joshua."

Arthur developed a cold feeling in his stomach.

"Say it, Alexis. Say whatever you're saying."

"Artie, I love you, but—"

"But what?"

"You need to move out, Artie. You're no good for the baby."

There it was, his tongue frozen, his heart filling his chest so it squeezed his lungs into airless organs incapable of powering speech. He wanted to tell her everything, to make her understand the enormity and consequence of an entire life, his son's life, rolling out before him and all the possible madly wrong turns it could take, all because Arthur failed failed failed to form a word of warning or wisdom or love.

There it was.

Love.

How can you ever make anyone know you love them? That was his doubt.

But his flat lungs wouldn't give him anything. His dead brain sputtered, and he stood mute before Alexis until finally turning from the room and charging down the stairs, his fists balled. He'd never—not ever, not in a million years—hit a woman, but Junie was edge-of-the-cliff close. She stood in the kitchen holding a bowl of something, mixing it with one of her funky spoons. She had that cow-eyed look, that slightly open mouth, down-turned. He'd never noticed how much he hated the shape of her mouth, which was not Alexis's mouth. That must have been from the phantom father who'd dissipated by delivery.

"You put this crap in her head," he said. "You wanted me out."

"This was all her idea." Junie hugged the bowl against her stomach. She stood in the center of his kitchen, Arthur's kitchen, which didn't smell or look like his kitchen anymore.

"She wants me to go," he said.

"Then maybe you should go. Maybe that thing will go with you." She turned and seemed to forget he was standing there. He took the booklet and the bottle of Balvenie and stepped out onto the patio.

He breathed in, out, in. He slammed the door behind him.

•   •   •

In the hardy twilight the woods beyond were holding something back. Arthur poured a long drink. Here he was again. Joshua was on his way, somewhere nearby, schlepping past trees, over logs, through stony rivulets, ready to emerge at any moment.

Arthur opened the booklet. *Sixty dollars*, he thought.

He read by the light of his phone. The information was mostly useless or repetitious. But he found something near the end. It said, "Travelers, if truly a product of psychic material, as some theories suggest, may only be the manifestations of individuals. Should one take this theory to its ultimate conclusion, it may be safe to surmise that, being the manifestation of *one* person, any given traveler may only exist *for* that person."

Arthur's heart bottomed out. Had he held back? It wasn't fair, was it? He'd read the baby books. Men couldn't feel the same way about their child until after it was born, couldn't love them in the same way a mother could. How dare anyone seriously expect that? Fathers didn't have the unfair advantage of a physical bond. They didn't grow the thing inside them or tear a piece of their own heartbeat away to lend it life, to jump-start the nebulous electrons building into a brain and nerves, spongy fingers, feet, penis. It wasn't fair, was it, to assume the traveler was his? Was Arthur's very own psychic dubiety made manifest?

But the unsureness was there, certainly, a pallid platform of shifting sand, and the confirmation of a traveler only reiterated this unease, this cyclical loop of questions about continuance, souls, morality, the whole barking madness of a world about to collapse, and him bringing another life on board, like dragging a drowning man into an already sinking lifeboat. Whatever the metaphor, he was unsure, and that shouldn't be punishable, not made visible because just now, of all times throughout history, of all the eras in which to exist, life's underside was suddenly displaying itself.

His drinking tonight was an angry, forced set of motions, finishing the glass and tipping the bottle to his lips, reasoning that the burn in his throat was somehow stripping him down, peeling his vacillation so it dropped into the acid of his stomach, so he could piss it out and be done with it by morning.

going anywhere

He waited and drank, and Joshua was very late that night.

• • •

A rustling in the trees drew Arthur up short. Joshua stepped forth. Seeing Joshua now, Arthur knew this: Joshua *was* to blame for Alexis's illness. He was anxiety embodied. Every cell of him Arthur had wrought from each finely tuned pause at the mirror to question his capacity to be a father, every flinch as he sat in a meeting flipping his pen, or every slow, self-imposed chiding on his drive home due to not having accounted for one more future expenditure, one more second of his son's life. Joshua was the insidious, the niggling, and the dark. And these parts of him were controlling the outcome of Alexis's pregnancy.

Arthur stumbled, carrying the whiskey toward the familiar figure hobbling across the lawn.

"I want to know how to get rid of you," he said. "I want you to go away. You're bad news."

Joshua didn't respond.

Arthur threw a phantom punch that came within an inch of Joshua's cheek. The thing didn't flinch. Arthur knew suddenly that Alexis had been right. Because if this walking corpse was Arthur's own anxiety, it was tied to everything else, too. To take a crowbar to it was to shatter all the psychic pieces that made up their dreams, their desires, all the parts that made up a child. To obliterate Joshua was to rob the flesh of its fantasy, of its elegant cosmic fortitude.

He screamed, tore through a flurry of punches, drawing up short, midair, half-wanting to make contact by accident. He howled, he swore, he kicked at the grass until the thing was out of sight, piercing the dark edge of the woods and sliding away into shadow.

Hours later, Arthur awoke on the lawn with the sun turning the dew to crystal.

• • •

Arthur resisted.

butterscotch

For another week he stood about after supper, hangdog, in his own living room. He'd begun eating by himself before the television in the den, the sound turned low, his eyes unfocused on the commotion of the screen while Alexis and Junie scraped and dipped and spoke in funereal whispers to one another over the table. Afterward, the act of having eaten apart seemed to facilitate a new isolation that found him shuffling around the coffee table, pretending to look at old family photos as if he were some vacuum salesman waiting for the interested wife who would be along shortly with tea. But Alexis never joined him, and he eventually stopped pacing, finally standing there, hands at his sides, considering the strange shape of this room with all these things in it and the way it held his tiny life so quietly.

He began packing his belongings.

He went to work and made blunders, spent hours fixing them, and found that the extra time away from the house appealed to him. So long as he stayed gone, Joshua might too.

He stopped looking for Joshua in the evenings, hoping his lack of interest would convince whatever psychic particles had coalesced into this being to disband. Whatever covalence had drawn them together was now moot, he thought, gone, a substanceless epicenter. He flushed his mind of doubts with positive thinking and meditation in his car at lunch and hoped Joshua would simply flitter away on his own.

But then Arthur, finally home, late in the evening, would be rinsing a plate in the sink and look out to see this being, trudging forlornly, hauling itself through the hostas.

•   •   •

One Sunday afternoon he gave up the fight. Alexis developed a fever, and Arthur toted his suitcases and toiletry bag to the car.

"I'll just stay in a hotel," he told Junie.

She didn't look up from her crocheting. Whatever she

was making had spiraled out in a patterned circle like a giant blue and red web on her lap.

"Just hope you haven't waited too long," she said.

• • •

He stayed for one last supper. He hadn't the heart to turn the television on, and he sat there at the edge of the couch chewing a piece of bleach-white bread, which was all he could keep down anymore.

Alexis and Junie retreated to the upstairs bedroom early, and Arthur found himself regretting that he didn't have a single utilitarian reason for tromping up there. Feeling the home-threads unraveling, he reached for the whiskey one last time and took it onto the patio. A part of him knew he might not even go back through the house when he left. He'd detour around the side of the garage. A part of him knew he might never see his wife again.

Joshua appeared somewhat later, and halfway through his ramble, Arthur rose and approached him one last time.

"What do you want?"

Joshua made no response.

"You talk to me, you son of a bitch. You give me the time of day."

Joshua didn't react. No change in course. Nothing.

Arthur moved closer to whisper into his ear.

"I'm going to get rid of you. I'm not leaving you here. You should know that."

Still nothing.

He'd never been this close. Arthur could smell him now, that crumbled-dust smell, wet ash, dry storm drains, neglected basements, rust. It was the scent of bloodless decay, the remnant of remnants left over in the ruin, an echo of death.

Arthur took a step back. He sniffed slowly. A new look was breaking across his face.

"You're as real as anything," he said. He threw the whiskey, glass and all, into the yard and headed for the house. Opening the door, he was met with that wall of butterscotch scent. He could hear Alexis upstairs, shuffling and sobbing, sobbing and shuffling.

Junie was back in the kitchen, mixing something new.

He moved toward her and she flinched, like he might pop her in the jaw. The bowl wobbled in her hand, almost slipped free. He didn't look at her. He plucked the four candles off the counter.

"Those aren't yours," she said.

"It's my goddamn house," he said. He was racing around the rooms now, the bottom of his shirt held up to form a basket in which he laid the candles—now the ones on the toilet, the end tables, those little shelves on the wall in the hallway. He was charging upstairs, searching them out, the nightstand, the bathroom windowsill.

He began arranging them, lighting them as he went, a few on the stairs, down the hallway, through the kitchen, out onto the patio, and into the soft grass of the yard. This trail of burning candles.

Junie followed him to the doorway. "You'll set fire to the whole house," she said.

Arthur lit the final candle. He placed it a couple feet from Joshua, who seemed especially slow this evening, especially reluctant to go.

"You're crazy," Junie shouted. "I have a mind to call the police."

She leaned over like she might blow out one of the candles on the patio, and Arthur smacked a fist into his palm to get her attention. "You blow that candle out, and I'll do the same to you."

It was a ridiculous thing to say. He didn't know what it meant, even, and it almost made him waver. The plan was stupid. The idea. But the threat did the trick. Junie rose up. Her face suddenly went slack. She backed out of the doorway and nearly tripped over her own feet. "Oh God," she said. "Oh God, what have you done?"

Arthur turned to see Joshua changing course, following the candles as an airless, dry moan escaped his gray lips.

He passed over or through the candles. His ashen legs brushed the flames and put them out as he went. The moaning grew louder, multi-voiced somehow, as if a choir had begun clamoring in the dust-softened halls of Joshua's throat.

By the time Joshua reached the door leading into the house, Junie had regained herself and was hunched over trying to blow another one out, but she was wheezing. She rose up full of scarlet in her cheeks, unsuccessful, holding her chest, then retreated to the living room where she swooned back on the couch in a sweat.

"You've done it now," she said as Arthur entered the room. Her face reversed its coloring and went fish-belly white. Her eyes rolled back in her head.

"I have," Arthur said.

Joshua lumbered down the hall, his features all the more broken and hideous in the artificial light of the house. The voices in his throat, for there were several, took over the rooms. It was the cold sound of water and wailing swirling together until it buzzed in Arthur's brain, vibrated in his bones.

"Why?" Junie wheezed.

Arthur took a seat beside her on the couch.

"He's inescapable," he said, and on cue the monster emerged into the living room, rounding the open doorway toward the stairs. "Maybe there are too many people in the world. Maybe there's too much bad psychic energy, like they say." He pointed at Joshua. "But he's not the past. He's not a ghost. He's our fear of everything—everything unsaid, undone."

Junie's eyes watered, her breathing shallowed out.

"You don't ever get rid of doubt or anxiety or fear or pain," Arthur said. He could smell it now, that scent of ash and death and burning gold leaves taking the summer away, same as autumn when Arthur was a child. And it was tempering the overly sweet butterscotch smell so that the air became a palpable, hot, living thing, a life laying itself across other lives, a breathing bold body in its own right.

butterscotch

"You don't get rid of all the bad," he said. He watched Joshua ascend the stairs that led to where his wife was lying in the bedroom. The candles snuffed out as he went, one, two, three. . . .

The voices were higher-pitched now, ascending with the stairs, growing, to Arthur's ears, angelic.

Junie slumped to the left and slid off the couch where she lay on the floor, weeping, blubbering.

Arthur could hear Alexis calling his name.

"All that bad stuff," Arthur said. "You learn to live with it."

snapshot of domestic scene with rescue dog

You read things like this occasionally. In the doctor's office. An article. Not in *People* or *Rolling Stone,* but *The International·Journal of Stress Management,* a drab, scholarly periodical which is certainly on the coffee table by mistake. A study was done. A new way for tabulating the pressures of everyday living. Do this, it said. Take one instant from any part of your day—a snapshot. Dissect and parse it until its myriad components reveal the sum of its surrounding influences: now you have a single life. One need only take the snapshot mentally and evaluate it later.

So the snapshot is this: a tidy living room and a television with the still image of a black-and-white movie. On screen is a forgotten starlet glowing through a fog filter. My husband, Arnold, stooping over the couch and swiping crumbs from the cushions. That's another part of the snapshot.

"It's your mother's fault," he says.

He whisks a nugget of feta cheese off the couch. Tonight I've been watching *Penny Serenade,* and I paused the film to go into the kitchen for pepper. I left the bowl of rigatoni

snapshot of domestic scene with rescue dog

right there on the armrest. The dog, a cocker spaniel-shepherd mix, can't be blamed. Not for taking the opportunity. Not for scattering the pasta and smearing the mushroom sauce across the throw pillows and carpet.

"Your mother always cleaned up after you," he says. "That's who I blame. You never learned cause and effect." Despite the speech, he's scrubbing the upholstery for the right to say he's done so. The dog, Betsy Blue, crouches near the door. The dog is another part of the snapshot. A rescue dog. That's what they called her. I hadn't heard that term until the adoption. I'd heard 'pound puppy.' 'Mutt.' 'Stray.' But rescue dog, that lent a heroic quality to things. Arnold and I—we *rescued* her, same as pulling her from a burning building.

The dog cowering in the corner. There's a detail with meaning. A *rescue* dog. More meaning. And me in the doorway to the kitchen. In the snapshot I'm positioned to the left according to the rule of thirds. I'm leaning against the doorjamb, and my dog is cringing off in a corner to the right while Arnold berates us both from the foreground. A snapshot. A life. All with meaning.

• • •

I watched Arnold from the kitchen doorway and knew I was leaving. Knew it for the first time with any certainty. He hadn't hit me, didn't drink heavily or cheat so far as I knew. In fact, he'd recently made associate professor and we celebrated the possibility of his tenure by paying forty dollars for a bottle of wine. But Arnold was convinced his career had stalled. He'd begun wearing frustration like a cologne. With his new insurance I'd gone for a wellness check at the ob/gyn. Then Arnold and I discussed children. We discussed his frustration. We adopted a dog. In that order.

And now, in my snapshot, I was a woman who knew she wouldn't be here tomorrow. I knew it the same way I knew my father was dead my senior year of high school. A silvery prescience descended over everything. That afternoon in late May a bottle-green sky had filtered down amid the firs of the private campus. I'd just scored a '*pass with honors*' on my microbiology exam and I'd been about to call home when the feeling settled across me like ash. I'd held my breath and counted to one hundred in my head as I sat down on the cool stone steps of the Sciences building, and all the world flattened out into a picture tinged with the wrong shades. By the time I reached my dorm my mother had deposited an incoherent message of shrill bleats into my answering machine. After that the machine became un-reliable, inadvertently erasing several messages from high-school staff whose careful voices died in the room's empty air. It was as if the machine, traumatized by the news, re-fused to remember any more.

But this moment with the feta and Arnold and the dog felt like a replacement photo, something you place on top of the other one, leaving the old one in the frame for safe-keeping, so only you can remember it's there. It had the same crisp edges, similar colors and composition, with the same sense of certainty.

Same as knowing my father was gone, I foresaw the events as they'd play out with Arnold. I'd sleep in the bed with him. He'd doze off and refuse to move toward me in the dark, making a show of holding his blanket so that I'd either have to draw closer or do without. I'd do without. In the morning I would arise and make my own breakfast. He'd be off by ten-thirty to teach class. Then quickly but calmly I'd gather my clothes, toiletries, three pairs of shoes, my basket of cherished greeting cards, the humidifier with the blue lid, my electric blanket, and a small igloo cooler full of snacks for the road. I'd limit my books to the gifted and nostalgia-laden—Plutarch's *Lives* from Eddie; an old copy of *Immortality* I bought in a gas station during a rafting trip to West Virginia; my father's *Old Man and The Sea*, so brittle it was unreadable without risk of serious damage; and, of course, the generic little collection of 1950s short stories my mother gave me when I was sixteen. Then I'd be out, on my way home to Indiana, the warm sunshine gliding across the sap-spotted window as I hummed along to the radio.

Neat as a bow on a boxed-up birthday gift, my mother would say. Another snapshot, I'd say. This one of freedom and unlimited potential.

* * *

Arnold deposited the handful of crumbled cheese into the trash, gathered up the dog's sheet, and stormed out to the garage where he made some noise with the washer lid. He trudged up to bed as I rinsed a few glasses in the sink, my swipes repeated over and over until I was certain he wasn't coming back.

My stomach grumbled, and I thought how nice it would be to quell my hunger tomorrow with a deli-turkey sandwich from the igloo cooler. Then I slipped a few more tentative titles forward on the bookshelf so they stuck out half an inch, and I gave Betsy Blue a slow stroke across her head. The dog seemed to like Arnold but to twitch and tremble when he raised his voice. We had no way of knowing what she'd been through.

The phone rang—it was the landline Arnold used as his contact for the university. I answered.

"This Samantha Kingsbury?" The voice was old and southern, tarnished brass on the syllables.

"Yes, who's this?"

"Peter Chynoweth. I'm brother of Elise."

"I'm sorry, I don't know any Elise."

"Maybe not, but she's your neighbor cross the way."

The name rang its distant bell. A small, elderly woman with a dented Camry that rolled out of its cavernous garage every Sunday morning—presumably for church. But the name Chynoweth didn't sound right.

"Oh," I said. "Is something the matter?"

"Fact, yes. Can't reach my sister on her line."

"Could she be out?"

"Not possible. Don't know as I want to make a federal

case out of the matter, so I was wondering if you might—"

"Can't *you* come? I don't mean to sound rude."

"I live in Tennessee. I call her Wednesdays. Clockwork."

"But how did you get my name? This is—I don't see how I could—"

"Google Maps street view. Figured out your address. Cross-referenced it with white pages. Looked you up. You're the second Kingsbury in the county."

I had no snapshot for Peter Chynoweth. The quaint vision I'd formed of a decrepit World War II veteran surrounded by his Reader's Digests, cat in his lap, hunched over a rotary phone in a moonlit cabin in Tennessee, crumbled apart. But I couldn't visualize the alternative either: the old man zooming in on my mailbox through the little digital window of his computer. For just a fleeting second I wondered who the other Kingsburys in the county were and if their lives were happier than ours.

"If you could just knock on her door. You'd be doing an old fella a mighty favor."

I heard myself say, "Okay."

He gave me his number with instructions to call collect so I wouldn't be charged long distance. I hung up the phone and gazed up the stairs, waiting for Arnold to cross from the bathroom to the bedroom, to ask about the call, but he'd already turned out the light.

I could have gone to get him. The distraction of trekking out together to check on an old woman might have broken our stalemate. My vision of the next morning would dissipate into a blurred watercolor of itself. And part of me thought this might be okay. Backsliding.

On the sideboard by the door were my keys. I held my breath, counted to ten. The surface of my tongue felt tingly, the way it does when I blow up balloons. Then the keys were in my hand, quietly clasped as I slipped outside.

• • •

Our little renovated farmhouse, which we had not been the

snapshot of domestic scene with rescue dog

ones to renovate, was situated in countryside that, for the most part, retained its bucolic roots. It's what had attracted Arnold and me to the place. Not too far from town, but rustic. A small, organic dairy farm was down the road. A piebald Holstein—painted on a yellow wooden sign—stared out at you with languid eyes as you rounded the bend. Further along, a Boy Scout camp lay hidden in the hills. And between here and there were only a few houses, either boxy little homesteads or the newer, roughhewn cabins, which were made to look comfortably ancient.

The old woman's house was about an eighth of a mile off the road at the end of a long gravel drive. The drive skirted a field which at this time of year was shoulder-high with green wheat. I angled the car into the gravel and stopped, taking in the dilapidated gate. It was permanently held open, overgrown with ivy, and there was a rusty mailbox with *PARTRIDGE* spelled out in neat black letters. Another snapshot.

Partridge. Not Chynoweth. I saw the mailbox at least three or four times a week and still hadn't been able to recall the name. As I moved up the drive my headlights felt out the angles of the house and surrounding nightscape. Shadows sprung to life against the nearby barn, a weather-eaten old hulk of chipped white paint with a green, aluminum roof. The place was old but well kept. Bushes of prim, Noisette roses swayed on either side of the storm door in clusters of white. I parked and stood in the moonlight. The silent gravel at my feet looked scrubbed and precious. It must have been going on nine, but the night felt older. If the woman were in bed, would I just be shaking her out of a sound sleep? Banging on the door seemed suddenly ridiculous and cruel, and I re-thought my promise to Peter Chynoweth. Let them sort it out in the morning.

Then I remembered Chynoweth's frankness and clarity. This, more than if he'd been blubbering with worry, gave credence to his concern. In the four years since Arnold and I moved out here, we'd never heard from Mr. Peter

141

Chynoweth. Not a peep. And my mind jumped to the in-fomercial for medical bracelets on late-night television in which a baritone voice lists all the medical maladies allevi-ated by quick response: stroke, heart attack, broken bones. I had a vision of frail Elise Partridge lying in her darkened kitchen awaiting help, knowing perhaps it might be days away—might, in fact, be too late.

Not a snapshot I wanted to imagine.

•   •   •

I climbed the old concrete steps, fissured with age, their surfaces sloping earthward, and stood in a kind of defen-sive stance before knocking. After several unsuccessful at-tempts I opened the storm door and pounded on the in-ner one, alternating between its wood and glass panels. I couldn't decide which made the louder noise. When that failed I moved to the side of the house. Cutting through the neat grass, I found a dirt path broken up by chipped flag-stones. More rose bushes, and I imagined them humming with bees during the day.

The house sat high on its foundation, and the bottoms of the windows were more than six feet off the ground, so I couldn't get a direct view into the rooms. I saw, at this an-gle, a ceiling with a darkened light fixture hanging from it, given shape by what I guessed was a blue stove light.

And like that I thought of another snapshot. My moth-er's kitchen after my father passed away. The stove light left on. My mother, a consummate eco-warrior, a woman who went around unplugging appliances with power-indicator lights because "even those use up energy," had never be-fore left a light on in the house. She'd taken Jimmy Carter at his word, she said, and had drilled the practice into us with such vigor that we often thoughtlessly flipped switches when exiting rooms, enveloping anyone still sitting there in darkness. After the funeral, that light over mom's stove cast its liquid shades over the still-glowing appliances, the kitchen chairs, the table. It imbued them with a kind of

stage presence. And it became a static essence that suggested stagnation. All could be inferred. A snapshot of a woman afraid. Of burglars. Of the world coming to a halt while
she wasn't looking.

For the next few years I came home during holidays and
part of my summers, but I didn't notice the light again until
Arnold—my second "serious" boyfriend—accompanied me
on the Christmas break before my final semester at Brown.
He'd undergone a mostly successful introduction to cousins
and aunts and grandparents, and the two of us had stayed
up in the den for a make-out session long after the others
had gone to bed. When Arnold went for a glass of water to
walk off some rising sexual tension, he'd come back with a
puzzled look on his face.

"Did you know your mom has puppets?"

He led me into the kitchen where only the stove light
still burned. Three bits of string had been taped to the vent
over the stovetop. From each string hung a piece of black
cardboard, each cut into a distinct shape.

"What the hell are these?" I said.

"I thought it was a joke."

The cardboard pieces were silhouettes. I could see it now.
I touched the largest one. It was a man. There was the ridge
of a collar, the protuberance of a tie's knot emerging from
his throat. The bottom of his slacks cut a neat line above his
shoes, which looked formal because of the notched heel.
He was dressed for work and seated but chairless, with a
cup of coffee halfway to his lips. The smaller two cutouts
were children—one a boy, the other a girl—and were like-
wise without chairs. The little boy had his hand raised, his
intricate little fingers splayed. His mouth was open as if
adamantly explaining something. And there was the girl,
whose head was bowed, perhaps in prayer, with both of her
hands held out flat before her.

They'd been stuck there a long time. The scotch tape
holding them to the vent was browned with age and food-
smoke and dust. The string was stiff, and the silhouettes

didn't flutter or spin. If I took a step to the right I could see that my mother had positioned them to cast shadows against the wall, forming an optical illusion that made it appear as if all three shadows were seated at the table. The man was my father, of course, a perfect, flat rendition. He was accompanied by me and Eddie as children, Eddie's spidery tousle of hair rendered piece by piece, probably from some home-movie still. My own expression had been recreated out of a shoe-box ether of memories. I hazily recalled a faded polaroid of myself in this pose, my meek smile evidenced in the appled curvature of my cheeks.

The fourth chair at the table was empty. I thought of my mother in the house alone, the days we had gone without talking stretching sometimes into months as I found myself more and more caught up with school and early job hunts and talks of engagement. I thought about Eddie, my brother, only two years younger and off encountering the world for himself.

• • •

I slid around the back corner of Elise Partridge's house. There I found a shabby set of wooden stairs. Hardy trumpet vines spilled over the pipe serving as a banister. A hummingbird feeder adorned the rusty light over the door, I knocked, and the syrup swooshed around inside its glass.

When I still got no answer I tried the knob and found it unlocked. I crossed through a screened-in porch. Its boards creaked nervously beneath my feet. The inner door was open to the night air, and I passed into the kitchen. At the table was an elderly woman, very short. Her toes in her black Velcro shoes barely reached the floor. Her head lay in her hands across the table. A blue and white plate with a fork and a few bits of dried food had been pushed to the left of her, a juice glass to the right.

A snapshot.

"Mrs. Partridge? Mrs. Partridge, are you okay? Oh, for Christ's sake."

144

snapshot of domestic scene with rescue dog

I wished I'd brought Arnold then. And I was mad at him for forcing me to leave. We'd made a life together, and it was about to be gone. I touched the old woman's shoulder and gave it a gentle shake. She didn't feel stiff, but she didn't move.

"Mrs. Partridge," I whispered, but it came out as the beginning of a sob.

The final photograph, I thought. The blue stove light casting its mysterious glow the way, it always did. The old woman alone. It was too easy for me to see myself and my mother here in this same pose. The same photo of death for each of us, and it made me want to weep, not just for Mrs. Partridge, but for all of us.

I used my cell to call 9-1-1 and settled into the chair beside Mrs. Partridge to wait. I was a mourner at a private wake, a woman in a kitchen, sitting with the dead, the way my mother did each evening. I'd never even asked her about the silhouettes. I hadn't known how to bring it up.

I looked around the kitchen, and there was another detail to Mrs. Partridge's snapshot, a black line of rot that had settled around the walls about six inches from the floor as if a flood had once filled the house. I imagined Mrs. Partridge alone, crying until salty tears made an ocean of every room and stirred up the basement like the bottom of a lake troubled by a storm. I thought of Mrs. Partridge's loneliness and what it must have been like, but all of it felt like abstraction, a remote *idea* of loneliness rather than its heart.

I was thinking of this kitchen. That kitchen. The undeniable theme of death slipping its way in through the hearth. Snapshots. Those stale roles of widow, wife, mother, doddering crone. Had I been trained to think this way? To sum things up like this? Was this the totality of life's incomprehensible and varied hues? I couldn't think of a single happy moment that wasn't eclipsed by this one still photograph: of a woman dead in her own kitchen while another woman sat there staring into space.

And suddenly the trip back to Indiana held no sunshine for me, didn't fill me with the same hope it had only a half-hour ago. I didn't want to think anymore. Thinking got you nowhere. Snapshots got you nowhere.

Then Mrs. Partridge kicked and I jumped in my chair.

"Holy shit holy shit holy shit," I said. I pushed at Mrs. Partridge's shoulders to right her in her chair.

Mrs. Partridge allowed herself to lean against the chair-back, waggling her jaw as if stiff.

"Well, what are you doing here?" she asked.

"I'm your neighbor."

"And you think that's a *good* explanation?"

I laughed. Mrs. Partridge was alive. She was, as they say, a firecracker.

"My brother. Peter," Mrs. Partridge said. "He called you, didn't he?"

"He was worried about you."

"Oh, pfaaww. He wasn't worried one damn bit."

"He was," I insisted. "He didn't have anybody else to turn to." I put my hand on my heart.

Mrs. Partridge tested her dentures with her tongue. "You know how many houses sit on this road? Twenty-seven within a two-mile radius."

"We seem so alone out here."

"Maybe for city. But that's not the point. Do you know how many of those twenty-seven houses my brother has called?"

I imagined Peter Chynoweth frantically scrambling over the images in Google Maps, scanning the county telephone listings. Avoiding the authorities, the emergency operators, anyone who could make an official pronouncement. Maybe it was his way of keeping death at bay.

"He must have been panicked," I said.

Mrs. Partridge wheezed out a laugh.

"Not at all, dear. And he didn't make all those calls to-night. He's been doing this for five years. And for the re-cord he's been pulling stunts his whole life. For the *record,* he's called twenty-four out of the twenty-seven houses. That's counting you."

"I don't understand."

"My brother," Mrs. Partridge said frankly, "is what you call a prankster. He likes sending folks over to the house half-asleep to scare the wool out of me."

"It's a joke?"

"No one ever accused you of being quick, did they?"

"I still don't understand."

"Proves my point."

"Does your brother really live in Tennessee?"

"Yes," Mrs. Partridge said.

"But this is a joke."

"It is," said Mrs. Partridge. "But do you know how many of those twenty-four people still visit me on a regular basis?"

"I don't."

Mrs. Partridge stood and walked the plate and juice glass to the sink. She spoke over her shoulder.

"Twelve. Exactly half. They check on me. Julie Barnhart and her two boys come just about once a week. Ronnie Carlisle drops by when he thinks of it, always brings donuts. I don't know if he thinks of me and then buys the donuts or if buying the donuts puts me to mind. I don't know how I got mixed up with donuts to begin with. There's the Atkinson's. They run the little garage up the hill. Their daughter has MS. I watch her sometimes."

"You didn't know any of these people until your brother—what?—prank-called them?"

"I didn't," Mrs. Partridge said. "I've only lived here six or seven years."

"We've lived here four," I said.

"Do you know Dr. Stevens? He's the one that sold your place."

"I don't really know anybody who lives here."

"I'll have to introduce you."

I stood. "I called the police. The ambulance."

"We'll explain it. They'll chide me and tell me to keep

147

my brother on a shorter leash. Coffee?" She gestured to an old percolator with a faceted orange light glowing faintly.

I sat back down. What would I tell Arnold? And then the thought came to me. I wouldn't tell him anything. He was asleep, and I wouldn't ever tell him about leaving the house and finding Mrs. Partridge dead and then not dead.

"I'll have a cup, yes," I said. "I'll wait till the ambulance gets here. If that's okay."

"I wouldn't have asked if it weren't."

Mrs. Partridge poured the coffee for both of us.

"I'm leaving my husband," I said. I hadn't meant to say it. "I still love him. He's a good man. But I'm leaving."

Mrs. Partridge placed a sugar bowl between us and handed me a spoon.

● ● ●

I pulled into our driveway after midnight. Weeds whistled in the wind. I tip-toed into the house and found it the way I'd left it. The soap-streaked glass I'd been washing and forgotten to rinse sat on the counter alone. I gawked up at the steps like a kid watching an acrobat. Something at the back of my mind was unraveling.

Betsy Blue pattered down the stairs, weaving from side to side in her sleepy way, her paws clacking lightly on the wood. The dog was part of the snapshot, but it could not be said to be a replacement for children. Not like one might think. The picture was more complicated than that. And we had not been heroic. Not really. The Humane Society had already rescued the dog. All I did was adopt it after a fight with Arnold over the timing of children, over my own aspirations to go back to school. I'd needed the dog more than it needed me, but that was not the sum of it. The dog was one part. And I was one part. But we would also change. Life would fiddle with meanings.

I scratched the dog's back between the shoulder blades and suddenly felt like running through the woods. I wanted to feel wild. To come out onto a moonlit field, my breathing ragged with exertion, to taste the goldenrod thick on the night air. I wanted something, and whatever it was I wanted it desperately. I held Betsy Blue's head between my hands and stared deeply into the dog's dark eyes, trying to convey how deep I felt at that moment, how full of everything, so full that I could hold onto life for centuries. The dog licked my face. My nose. My cheeks. And I began to laugh.

"You're right," I said.

I pulled my cell phone from my pocket and dialed. I stared at my mother's number. I knew the night seemed to be begging me to call and close some loop. A snapshot of women in kitchens, I thought, and I sat at my own table. Bull shit, I thought. Somewhere along the line I'd begun to see life in terms of its patterns, no matter how cliché.

Mrs. Partridge hadn't lived her whole life on the farm. She wasn't dead. She didn't even seem lonely. Her snapshot in the kitchen was one of those things people like me imbued with meanings without ever sipping the coffee or touching the chipped little edge on the teacup above the rim.

And right then I felt like lying. Sending Peter Chynoweth's prank onward like a hot potato.

I erased my mother's number on the phone and dialed another. I heard our own landline ringing and finally Arnold's sleep-gravelled voice as he answered the phone.

"Hello?"

I dug low for my best baritone. My version of the man in the infomercial about strokes and heart attacks.

"Mr. Kingsbury?"

"Yes. Who's this?"

"I'm afraid your wife is dead," I said. "Killed in an auto accident."

I felt a silence sluice down through the house from the bedroom at the top of the stairs. I stood up quietly with the dog at my side.

I waited.

I waited for Arnold's steps on the floor above. Waited for

his frantic fumbling for a pair of jeans. Awaited the sound of him gathering his shoes near the closet. His shape as he descended the steps.

I waited.

I waited to see his face when he saw me standing here. Alive.

straw man

Idris bin Fartuwa is in danger of being left behind. Under the morning sun, the other merchants' camels already jangle with panniers of kola nuts, ostrich feathers, muskets, wax, copper, ivory, spice, and salt. Cowrie shells rub and rasp in their sacks. Slave rows, dark and ragged, lurch forward to the whip.

Near Kanem-Bornu last evening a camel in Idris's train keeled softly into the sand. With a foolishness brought on by exhaustion, he put off transferring its load until dawn. He is in a sweat now, harried, troubled. In his haste he has shifted the goods onto one camel rather than evenly dividing them between the other twenty-eight. The camel with the doubled load groans and spits furiously. Idris spits back and slaps its matted hide.

In place of the dead camel's carcass is a dried slurry of blood like a shadow without a reason. The surrounding plain teems with opportunists—cheetahs, leopards, genets, painted dogs. This also happened to his cousin, Ibn Battuta, snatched away by the silent jaws of some great beast. In

the gathering light Idris surveys the millions of wind-sharp-
ened rocks littering the valley like coarse salt and remembers Battuta's vital fluids seemingly strewn across each jagged one, his body scattered from Mali to Djeddha. Idris
has no intention of suffering the same destiny. Safety in
numbers. He will stay with the train and post his tent close
to the fire. But only if he keeps up.

His train surges past the spent firepits, and time seems to
slow down as Idris spots a single piece of wheat languishing
in the slope of a westerly dune. Lying there untrodden, its
slender, elegant stem and fanned head of golden kernels
suddenly represent to Idris all his life's struggles. His very
fate seems to hinge on its survival. Or perhaps, after all this
work, he simply can't bear to leave it behind.

He plucks it off the ground and shuffles up next to the
belly of his camel. Its hips roll achingly beneath the weight
of its new load. The goods on its back are no better secured than a pile of autumn leaves. Between a sack of grist-
ed grain and a reed basket he places the wheat, releasing it
with the delicacy of an artist finishing off the last stroke of
a masterpiece.

He hears a fleshy, hard snap, like a log being broken
beneath the wheels of a cart. The camel shits enormous-
ly, wails. A gruel-thin slurry of blood and yellow phlegm
shoot over its tongue past its bared teeth. Legs buckle. The
neck strains. The camel collapses. Its back has been broken
by the last straw, the way it was when Clarence Pasternak
walked into his government job in Seattle, Washington, sat
down at his desk, pulled open his filing cabinet, and found,
nestled within his manila folders, a human turd.

●　●　●

Six months after the turd incident Clarence Pasternak carries a severed hand in a brown, scabbed suitcase through
the parking lot of a two-story motel. The motel, which looks
like a shabby papier mâché version of other shabby motels,
sits off the I-30 south of Dallas in a night still as a crime-

scene photo. With none other than his mortal soul at stake, Clarence stalks up the crumbling cement stairs.

The exterior door of room 207 holds itself together with numerous layers of flaking paint so multi-hued they don't so much emit the color red as suggest it. The air is heavy for a Dallas night, mercury has plummeted in every barometer over three counties, and evening thunderclouds have dropped like a cork over the city. Clarence checks the armpits of his shirt in his sport jacket. Light spotting. He smells the nasturtiums in the flower beds below, someone's attempt to add color to the place, though the blooms resemble fizzled firecrackers in a limp sky.

Jenna Travoli answers on the third round of knocks. A short woman, thirty-four, with heavy black ringlets that pour around her shoulders like smoke from a burning tire, she puts a hand on her hip.

"Who are you?"

Clarence has shaved his eyebrows in accordance with the clerical law of the Church of Your Holy Humble Tattered Sail, or CYHhTS (novitiates call it "Chits," as in the Church of Chits, which is redundant, like "ATM machine"; or themselves "Chit-lings," usually with a titter). As a result of his hairless brow, Clarence often looks surprised, the face of a dimwit observing a train wreck. Jenna Travoli responds the way most people do, which is to raise her own eyebrows, as if being astounded together they might find a common expression.

"Jenna?" says Clarence. "Clarence Pasternak. From high school. Do you remember me?"

A bombardier beetle, with a snappy fart of its wings, threatens to enter the apartment. Jenna closes the door and steps forward. She and Clarence look as if they might waltz.

"What happened to your eyebrows? Were you in a fire?"

"No. I just wanted to tell you sorry."

"How did you find me?"

That wasn't easy. Most people—internet search. Facebook,

MySpace, People Profile—the usual cybernetic midden heaps. But with Jenna, he got the sense she moved around, didn't live what you'd call a stable life, to which her accommodations testify with a very big raised hand and a hallelujah, thank you Jesus.

The short answer as to how he found her was a private detective and $1200. Not the kind of information you offer up.

"I just came to apologize," he says. "We went out on a date in high school. Remember?"

"Are you stalking me? Fuck, man."

"No—just—we went on a date. I took you to the movies."

"What was that? like fifteen years ago?"

"Sixteen," he says. "The movie was—"

"*Babe.*" A quick smile cracks the corners of her mouth.

"No. At least I thought it was *Braveheart.*"

"Never seen it. Maybe I saw *Babe* with my little sister."

"You've never seen *Braveheart*? Mel Gibson with the blue face—"

"So you're stalking me. I'm flattered, I am." She eyes him head to toe. "I'll fuck you for like two hundred dollars. That's an 'old-friends' rate."

"Are you a prostitute?"

"No," she says. Her tone is grimly ambiguous. "But I'll fuck you for two hundred dollars."

It crumbles: this picture he's constructed from memory of the two of them, teenagers, sitting in the back row of the cheap Marquee Theater downtown.

"Look, I just wanted to say sorry. I was seventeen. Not that my age excuses anything, but I was horny. I grabbed your"—looking at them now he feels self-conscious—"breasts. I got the sense you weren't into it, but when we were holding hands I put your hand—on my—crotch."

She giggles. A snort. "This is an AA thing?"

"Not AA. But, I have to say sorry."

"God, do you know how many guys—you know what, never mind." She rests her hand on the knob. "So give me two hundred dollars."

"I don't want to sleep with you."

"That deal's off. If you're so sorry, give me two hundred dollars. We'll call it even."

• • •

Less than an hour later Clarence enters a bar, his briefcase cutting prow-like through the crowd. He reaches the Radcliffes at a small table near a tinted window. They are a quiet couple in their early thirties sipping martinis and Clarence greets them by forming a baby wave with his left hand.

"Holy Christ!" John Radcliffe stands up and clamps onto Clarence's shoulder.

About nine years ago, before the human defiling of his filing system, Clarence met John Radcliffe in a government office that smelled of canned corn, its overly starchy miasma sweet as the stench of apricots in baby vomit. As one of the civil servants employed in this office Clarence handled applications for disability benefits and government aid for job training. Most of the people Clarence saw in a day would—whether as a result of environment, lack of opportunity, or sheer laziness—never amount to anything.

John Radcliffe, on the other hand, was a young man far more in control of his life than Clarence thought possible at twenty-three. John worked as a summer-job coach for underprivileged teens, which meant he *volunteered* his time, helping high school kids who were painting yellow curbs realize that their futures didn't have to end on the high school drop-out list. And while Clarence lingered for another eight years at this job with the baby-spew smell and the forlorn, weary-eyed people, eating up his twenties in a single, sour-breathed gulp, John Radcliffe moved on to medical school, completed his residency and took up other forms of charitable dispensation, all while maintaining an enviably compact physique and pliant flair for yoga. Clarence's revenge had been to sleep with his wife.

John kneads a thumb into Clarence's trapezius.

"Clay, how you been, man? What are the odds?"

155

going anywhere

The odds are high. Private detective—$700: *'Radcliffes: Weekly to bi-weekly nights out, Fridays or Saturdays, around nine or ten, at the Mirabel Lounge. Not far from Subject 17 (Jenna Travoli).'*

"God, I don't know, man. You still in Dallas?"

Emma simulates a hug. "Why are you here?"

"Bit abrupt," John says.

In a last-minute bout of vanity, Clarence has quickly pasted on two fake eyebrows—a quite real-looking set for which he paid heftily at a 7th Avenue boutique. He nervously touches them both.

"Don't say anything important," John says. "I'm getting us another round."

For a moment, alone, Clarence and Emma stare at one another.

Their indiscretions numbered seven in all. The first time took place a year after John and Clarence met. John had moved to Dallas to begin medical school, leaving his bride of seven months to deal with the logistical details of transporting their possessions from point A to point B. She'd called Clarence three days into a packing nightmare of brown boxes that looked to have multiplied like tribbles, half-full and nested across a plain of scattered belongings throughout the house. She was sobbing.

That afternoon he helped her sort kitchen utensils from sheafed notes about cellular biology. As a respite, he took her out that evening to the party of a friend, which degenerated quickly into an empty kitchen, shoddy stereo rattling like a loose muffler as the host sang alone to Ace of Base's *The Sign.* They slipped out, too ashamed to say their goodbyes, and in the hallway Clarence noticed that Emma, perhaps in a fit of commiseration with their host, had consumed too much alcohol. On the walk home he had the giddy sensation that when she brushed his hand it wasn't a drunken blunder. When she leaned toward him, Clarence mentally chanted over and over, *She's drunk she's drunk she's drunk,* until her lips came into contact with his own, wetting his mouth with a simple sweetness that poured into his body and enveloped him in a cotton candy cocoon.

"He knows," she says. "That's why he just left. Are you happy?"

Clarence opens his mouth, but all the opening lines die on his tongue.

"I told him two years ago. He wanted to kill you. When he found out, he wanted to fly out to Seattle and beat you with a baseball bat. He was going to check it at the airline."

Even Clarence's thoughts are stammering. He searches for a way to begin, but Emma keeps talking.

"He'll murder you—I mean it—tonight if you don't leave right now. I'll tell him you had something come up. Just put your phone to your ear and walk out. Simple as that."

"I have something to say—"

"You don't get to say anything. You have to go. He's coming."

Clarence fumbles for the phone in his pocket, pulls it out upside-down and slaps it to his face as he shoves through the sweat-sour crowd. Outside, the muggy air fills his lungs. His head swims. He gropes for his knees, bends over and dry-heaves in the parking lot. Then he flees like the coward he knows himself to be.

He's on the highway before he realizes he's left the suitcase behind.

•   •   •

When he was nine years old Clarence was a friendless chubby child with a buttery gob of chin that stuck out from his pale cheeks. Despite a sixth-grade growth spurt on the horizon, his present crying jags and equally ample hindquarters earned him the name "Blubberbutt"—or, for purveyors of titular etiquette, "Sir Blubberbutt the Fatass Homo." Under this barrage of invectives hurled sometimes from bus windows, across streets or down alleyways, Clarence eschewed all the most efficient routes to school, traipsing an extra two miles along the eastern row of gutted shops, graffitied storage units, and lively check-cashing establishments to finally pass a row of liquor stores before arriving home—a path which never lost him, God-be-thanked, a single lunch-money dollar or, God-be-damned, a single pound.

It was on one of these treks as the afternoon dimmed to the color of a dirty dime that Clarence saw the dog. A piebald mutt not more than six-months old with a shortened collie face and white paws, it was tied with patio-furniture webbing to a rusted standpipe in an abandoned lot. The pup had circled the pole to the webbing's limit and now had one side of its head pinned as if it were listening to secret sounds in the sewers below. Clarence caught sight of the dog as it leapt up in a last ditch effort at freedom. Its makeshift leash snagged a bur in the pipe. Its front paws dangled a few inches off the ground. Its breath rasped in its throat. Its back legs scrambled.

Clarence waddled toward it. The dog's previous owner had scrawled on a discarded VCR box, "DOG. FREE."

Clarence never owned a dog. Didn't know if this one would bite him. Its ladder of a rib cage heaved in and out as it swung its head from side to side, attempting to back out of its trap, which only garroted its neck more tightly.

Paralysis percolated up Clarence's legs. Some depthless panic ossified every inch of his muscles. The dog whimpered and wheezed. It whined. Its dark eyes bulged. Clarence was about to see it die.

This turned out to be the closest moment in Clarence Pasternak's life to a miracle. A promise to her own parents had led Clarence's mother into the half-hearted formality of hauling Clarence down to the occasional Easter Sunday service. These often sweaty forays in his ill-fitting suit had bred no intimacy between himself and the holy spirit. But right now, standing before this dying puppy with its jowls working slowly up and down, all Clarence could think to do was pray. Pray that somehow the animal exist beyond this moment.

A second after he hurled this request in the general

direction of heaven, a heavyset man, face like a plate of poutine, rounded the corner with a bottle of liquor in his hand and sneered. The man was ugly in multifarious ways—boiled toes with skin peeled back in ashy flakes that poked out from a dirty pair of sandals; moley nose; clapboard row of uneven teeth; spittle foaming white as frog's eggs in the corners of his mouth. But he possessed a pair of iron hands thick as mangled machinery.

"Hell, boy," he growled as he saw the dog. "You do that?"

Clarence shook his fat head.

"Damn," said the man. He set the gin bottle gently against a clump of grass. It leaned there as if displayed for a photo shoot, no bag, the tidy warder on the label striding out like an explorer emerging from the surrounding jungle.

The man laid a hand on the top of the dog's head, kneading the fur and wriggling his fingers beneath the taut line. It took him a moment. He breathed heavily through his nose. His elbows jutted out. His neck tensed. The muscles in his shoulders trembled. Then Clarence heard the piano-wire pop of the line as it snapped. The dog dropped to its front paws and wagged its head in the dirt. The man looked at the VCR box, gave another disgusted *hmmph*, and left with his gin in tow.

Clarence leaned over the dog. He started by rubbing the pink collar of mangled fur. The effect was minimal. The fur looked the way Clarence's cowlick did at the top of his crown when he tried to tame it. It was the first time he'd petted a dog without the nervous eye of his mother cutting him short.

The two of them walked home in silence.

His mother wasn't an animal lover, but neither was she immune to a heartfelt story of redemption. Clarence convinced her to keep it. Alex P. Keaton became Clarence's only friend throughout his lonely fourth grade year, awaiting him in the paneled hallway of their two bedroom apartment where Clarence's mother dished out a bowl of water before she left for second shift at Gino's Frozen Foods. It had a been a strain, keeping the dog, and Clarence would forever wonder what his mother did for the harsh-talking Slovak landlady to convince her to allow them the pet. But it was a hardship the two of them bore together, and the dog repaid in kind, stretching itself across the center cushion of their couch to act as a conductor between boy and mother in those important years when cuddling was becoming more awkward but no less needed.

Alex P. Keaton didn't live long—four years. He was struck by a Jeep one night near the house. The woman who'd been driving apologized tearfully and helped Clarence carry the still-breathing Alex inside the apartment. The dog seemed to recover for a few hours, the nasty gash above his left eye beginning to clot, but he slipped away in his sleep.

Clarence cried for weeks, but his transition from a pudgy kid to a somewhat gawky pubescent had been made, and Alex P. Keaton had seen him through it. That short prayer to a nebulous God had yielded results with a power beyond Clarence's expectation or comprehension. From that one prayer had come an answer that saw him over the rough waters of adolescence, long enough to launch him into the less awkward years when his body caught up to the sports being played, the girls being eyed, and the swaggers being exhibited.

Into adulthood he continued then to think of prayers with an economist's sense of currency, their potency and power in direct relation to their rarity. People who prayed daily were squanderous mints printing money that lost value with every kneel and murmur. Thus it happened that Clarence Pasternak didn't pray again until he was thirty-two, at the end of a long week in a thankless, government job which had ground him to a nub, and mashed that nub into a last floundering pancake of his soul.

● ● ●

That's when, six months ago, Clarence finds human feces in his filing cabinet, compliments of an unsatisfied client of the state government for which he works. It is the crowning moment in a long, unsatisfying, downwardly spiraling stint as a public servant, and before the janitor can even be called, rubber gloves donned, vom-sorb dispensed, he is gone out to lunch, never to return—because this is a tipping point, some last moment of wasted time wiling away his vital hours culminated in one heaping, steaming excretion of indignity.

He spends the rest of the day pacing between Pike Place Market and Pioneer Square, dodging tourists and reacquainting himself with the dank smell of the ever-rotting wharves. In the park he tries drumming up some brisk sense of the sea, turns his face to the dull salt air rolling off the sound as if it were a murderous squall. Yet nothing imbues life with meaning nor rekindles the completely mundane and acceptable fog in which he's been living. No brine cakes his skin. No fierce wind rolls down out of the north to try and take him. He is simply a little man on a big planet dying slowly.

In a last ditch effort at redemption he prays for the first time in over two decades. It is a simple prayer uttered in the familiar tone of a man seeking a personal favor. One line uttered to God:

Save me.

As night comes on Clarence wanders down a side street to a church where he hears parishioners singing hymns. The Church of Your Holy Humble Tattered Sail. A tidy, white building with corners as crisp as a Shaker-style outhouse. Forty-watt bulbs beam from interior fixtures with a dimness reminiscent of movies about older times.

The church in its pristine posture, frames the faces of its parishioners. They look small and doll-like through the windows.

• • •

The hand in the suitcase was previously the property of Belinda Montag of Santa Cruz County, California, two miles out of Salinas. Thirty-six-year-old Belinda, dead of a vascular occlusion in the Circle of Willis, had donated her body to "science," signing over all rights to a medical supply subsidiary owned by one Carl Overhoffen, devotee of, you guessed it, the San Fernando-based chapter of Chits.

Amputating the hands of cadavers and hiding their absence in a carnival parade of complex government documents, then rerouting them through the Willed Body Program of UC, San Francisco had become something of a specialty with Overhoffen, and by the time Clarence received Belinda Montag's carefully preserved hand, the water and fatty tissue replaced by a mixture of acetone and epoxy resin that would outlast a plastic bottle in any landfill, Overhoffen had been efficiently trucking handless cadavers to medical programs all along the west coast for going on nine years.

The Chit-lings viewed this body-part-carrying as a right of passage. "Hand-holding," they called it. Communion with the dead. As a novitiate of this generally under-scrutinized sect, Clarence carried his newly gifted hand with him wherever he went—that was the deal. But now. Now he'd lost it. And should he not show up to claim it, should Emma or John Radcliffe take his suitcase home and open it, scrutiny would not bode well for the Chit-pit.

In a Dallas parking lot with a view of the High 5, Clarence sits on the hood of his car contemplating his options. On top of the loss of the hand, he hasn't accomplished his mission: to apologize to Emma. More importantly, to apologize to John. Honesty, the Chit-lings are taught, is the core value of family, and like the top of a pyramid, honesty subjects its healing properties down and outward, providing a renewed foundation from which all living must proceed.

Before he can misplace the nerve, Clarence drives to the Radcliffe's and stands looking over their spacious lawn. Two primly maintained flower beds flank the sidewalk to the front door. The house lies dark, and Clarence feels his sense of propriety slipping. Does John really know? And if so, can Clarence imagine being bludgeoned to death by a baseball bat? If not, is it Clarence's right to break up a family? Wisdom says, if the Radcliffes love one another, they'll get through this, but something about the sleeping windows and quiet rooms fill Clarence with the kind of uncertainty that comes with silence.

It's very late. His thoughts feel heavy, his sense of the world distant and hazy.

One thing is certain. Short of an apology, Clarence needs that hand.

He creeps along the house hoping against motion sensors. Through a bay window in the breakfast nook he sees his suitcase sitting on the counter.

It is open.

•   •   •

Clarence touches the latch on a pair of moon-white French doors, and the right one swings open on a squeakless hinge. He removes his shoes, stoops into the kitchen on stockinged feet, and checks the case. The hand is gone. He pushes further into the house. No television. No talking. Must be going on two a.m. by now, and he feels his breathing bottom out. He's moved into the living room when he sees the small figure of a girl standing near the sofa. She is maybe four or five years-old. In her hand she holds Belinda Montag's bodiless one. It is a nightmare vision, that of a girl whose mother has just stepped on a land mine. The child makes no noise. She simply stares at Clarence in his ridiculous fake eyebrows and ankle socks.

He approaches her as stealthily and unmenacingly as possible, crouching as he holds out his hands.

"Do you mind if I have that?"

She draws it to her chest like a teddy bear.

"It's just, I left this with your mom and dad. Did *they* open it, do you remember?"

She shakes her head.

"Did *you* open it? Maybe after they went to bed?"

She nods.

"You're not in trouble. I just really need it back. I could—would you like some money? I could pay you for finding it. You could buy something."

She retreats to the foot of the stairs, still clutching the hand, her chin on the severed end.

"Wait," he says.

She clumps up a few steps. She doesn't take her eyes off him. She might scream, he thinks.

"I'm with the police. I just . . . need that."

Then he lunges. He grabs for the hand, but the girl is quick. She bounds up the stairs. He tears after her, trying not to think of getting shot.

She's at a dead run now. Her tiny feet pad up the steps. Clarence takes them in twos. She dashes around a corner just as he hits the landing. He is behind her in half a second, but she slips him and takes a hard left into a darkened room.

He follows.

Three feet into the room he stops. He waits for his eyes to adjust.

•   •   •

The story of Idris bin Fartuwa ripples out of the dark Sahara into history, traversing six hundred years until it becomes light as a feather, a simple phrase off-handedly dispensed.

The last straw, they say.

The unmitigated desperation. The braided acts of a single life reaching their nadir. When something has to give.

For Clarence Pasternak that moment was not, after all, the day he discovered a turd in his filing cabinet. Instead, it is the moment he finds himself chasing a nameless five-year-old through another man's otherwise sleepy home.

The straw that broke the camel's back, they say.

For Herbert Danton that moment was in June of 1897 when he gave up on the photography of spirits as a way of communing with his departed mother. In his earlier life, at the age of twenty and one, Danton had argued horribly over the dispensation of his father's estate. A wayward gambler, Danton delivered a bilious polemic in his mother's sitting room, then stormed out of the house, found the nearest saloon, and progressed with a legendary drunk that ended in a fistfight with a cow. For her part Mrs. Charles Rocforth Danton retired to her parlor in tears and fell asleep reading her Psalms; then, around three in the morning, she sponta- neously combusted, leaving a silhouette of pepper-colored cinders on the divan.

Danton's immense guilt over this event transformed him into a teetotaling lawyer and civil servant who retained ties to the old country out of respect for his mother's family in Ballyshannon—which was how he came to be council for William Makepeace Tattersall. Tattersall had been banished from Dublin for questionable practices with unearthed corpses. Excised from his share in the family's renowned horse-trading business, he eventually washed up with the rest of the world's refuse at the end of destiny's trainline, in California, where he spent the next odd decade working in an abattoir and writing tracts defending what the courts had called his 'unhealthy preoccupation' with the dismem- bered dead. Upon Tattersall's death these tracts reached Danton's office the same week he renounced the possibility that a tintype could capture his mother's ghost and there- by provide him with some proof that she'd forgiven him. A simple phantasmic gesture, a smile for instance, would have sufficed.

Tattersall's scribblings advocated a very real belief in the resurrection of flesh, and Danton latched on to this idea with the fervor of a novice. A way to mend otherwise unmendable relations. He erected the first Church of the Holy Humble Tattered Sail in Seattle, Washington in 1906, replacing Tattersall's grizzled image with that of a boat tossed in the storm, awaiting God to part the thunderheads. Aside from its mainstay congregation in Seattle, the church created a satellite ministry in San Bernardino, of which

Chester Montauk was a member. Montauk happened to be the great-great-great-grandfather of Belinda Montag, the woman whose hand now floated somewhere in the darkness before Clarence's blinded eyes. We are all connected.

Clarence stands in the soundless velvet of this room without light, his hands outstretched, his nerves crisp to any sensate perception of movement. He hears his own breathing and the unsteady weight of his own body on the floorboards. Was that him making that noise, or the child? Or someone else?

"Hello?" he whispers.

[The truth is that Danton's religion still relies heavily on the Biblical reanimative precedent of Lazarus and Jesus himself—Frankenstein has always been popular reading among its parishioners—though interpretation runs decidedly against the grain from dominant theological thought.]

Clarence leans out into the darkness, hoping to encounter a solid object, maybe the foot of the little girl's bed.

[Truth is that the Holy Humble Church of the Tattered Sail has always been made up of people like Clarence, lost in the usual ways.]

Clarence inches forward.

[Truth is these people trade casserole recipes during potlucks and talk about their children, taking comfort, not in doctrine, but in one another.]

Two quick steps, before he loses his nerve. His fingers come to rest on something warm.

[And while no member of Chits has ever been resurrected, they find a community. They find family.]

The flesh beneath Clarence's palm is not the shoulder of a small child, but the muscular thigh of a grown man. Somewhere in the dark, John Radcliffe laughs in a low, sleepy way.

Clarence lifts his hand, and John moans pitiably.

"Ah, babe, you started this. Don't stop now."

Clarence can make out the shape of John's body rolling toward a smaller one, Emma's.

166

"Babe?" John whispers.

Clarence for one horrible moment can think of only one thing to do. He searches his brain for other options.

"Babe?"

Clarence reaches over John, clasps Emma's wrist, lifts her arm, and lays it gently on her husband's thigh.

"Babe," John says in a satisfied tone.

The black shape of Emma Radcliffe shifts toward her husband. John kisses her lightly. Clarence hears it. She groans softly, then recognizes his advances. Sleepily, she kisses him back.

Clarence remains still. Every muscle in his back holds rigid.

The husband and wife come to life beneath the sheet, slowly at first. Then Clarence hears Emma release a giggle unlike any he's ever heard her make, even in their most fervent moments.

Life proceeds.

John and Emma Radcliffe making love while somewhere very close to the side of their bed hovers Clarence Pasternak and maybe a little girl with Belinda Montag's severed hand in her own.

Family.

Clarence has no idea how long the lovemaking lasts or how long he stands, breathless, afterward, thanking God that neither of the Radcliffe's require a post-coital bathroom break. He never relocates the girl, and he slips down the stairs through a house already turning cottony gray with morning.

•   •   •

In the morning light he is born anew, cradled in the fog of a dreamy sunrise blurring the hills beyond the Radcliffe lawn. Why change what isn't broken? Why look for life in the dead? Clarence finds his car parked badly near the curb and drives away. The invisible thread of belief between him and that dead hand pulls taut and finally snaps somewhere near Denver. From what he's seen, there's something in the darkness he's been missing and it has something to do with love. He wants to spread it around, tear it apart, and examine it more closely, but he can't. Instead he meets a woman in the church a month later. They date for one year exactly, through no prescribed rules but their own. Her name is Kathleen, and he proposes to her in front of her favorite bookstore, then goes through a rough time looking for a new job. Then he feels that lovely darkness rising up around his feet again, feels the world expanding and loosening up when he finds out Kathleen is pregnant. Because sometimes it's a good thing that not much matters in the world, that the whole damn place has become numb to its own idiosyncrasies and horrors. And now in his nightly walks down the wharf, the sense of impending doom lifts off the low sea as each day no phone call comes from the Dallas County sheriff's office or the state rangers, and Clarence breathes just a little easier knowing he's grown into living, knowing he had to. He explains this one day to his infant son, Alex, with the story of a man crossing the desert.

Clarence mimics the merchant sitting on the dune with his head in his hands to show the child what desperation looks like. Because Clarence has been thinking about what a man does when he's reached the end and there's nothing left to do but give up or lift the world in all its heaviness with your own two hands. He's been thinking about family. He's been thinking about what you learn from a moment like that, in the loving darkness of another man's home. He's been thinking about this story he has going in his head about this guy riding across the Sahara in a camel train, about reaching that point where something has to give. And he's been thinking the story can't just end there.

"Would you like to know?" he says to his son in that voice that's frankly getting a little annoying to Kathleen in the kitchen as she heats the bottle over the stove.

"He got up," Clarence says. "The merchant got up and he started walking. He left that stuff, that piece of wheat, left it all behind." And—because this is a child's story, after all; a lesson and a moral—the last few words he says in a rising pitch so as to draw a widening, toothless, slobbery smile from his boy

"And he never even looked back."

murray

I

At some point in the seven-hour drive from our home in Chapel Hill, I roll through the blue-green mountains of West Virginia and rehearse: "Murray, this is the last time." My hand rises off the wheel. Murray only understands simple, declarative sentences: "That's not a toilet."—"9-1-1 can track your phone."—"Bareknuckle boxing isn't a sport." That sort of thing.

Around three in the afternoon I arrive in Wellston, Ohio, an old iron town buried back in the Appalachian foothills. The main street is a strip of county road with a two-pump gas station and a few decrepit shops on either side. The shops' sun-faded signs offer bicycle repair and sewing supplies, nothing useful. I've been here twice: once to post Murray's bail; another to personally deliver a check to his old landlord. Not trips I'd have made under normal circumstances, but Beth asked.

I made my money the old-fashioned way: designing a

website linking rosters of high school alumni with public incarceration records. It's called ClassAFelons.com. People love it. They scroll back through the yearbook photos, click on the thumbnail of the guy who sat behind them in biology. You know the guy—the one who brought in his own frog to dissect and bragged about having sex with a distant aunt. Or the girl sitting in front of the laser background with the Aqua Net pompadour and braided mullet. People love taking bets on misdemeanors or felonies or no record at all—we have a separate tracker so you can see how many times people have guessed one way or the other. We also have a bevy of legal loopholes, public domain defenses, and safeguards developed by a firm we now have on retainer to keep us in business. A well-managed stock portfolio and what continues to be lucrative adspace do the rest. But Beth was before all that.

When I met Beth I was poor and soon to be jobless. I'd been managing network systems for a small credit union being swallowed by BankofAmerica. Despite the old adage that "I-T spells IN," I was out the first round of personnel cuts. So I drove my rust-punched Hyundai to a developer's conference in Milwaukee to sniff out opportunities, finagling my way into a cocktail party full of investors.

Beth, a French 75 in one hand, stood in the center of the room, back straight, bobbed dark hair, black dress, pearls. By then she'd earned her master's degree in public affairs from Wisconsin and traveled extensively in Europe. Along the way she'd coordinated a vaccination campaign against Marburg fever in Angola and picked up a passable Portuguese. She could recite Blake at the drop of a blue-crab croquette. I don't know what vintage wine it was that instilled in me the courage to talk to her, but I've looked for it ever since.

Our conversation was a success because Beth made it so. If she were the world-renowned cellist, I was the chimpanzee trying to mimic the movements of her bow. A million times since—in the nine years during which we've managed to date, marry, and do a few other things—I've asked myself: why would a woman like that give a guy like me the time of day?

The answer is simple: Murray.

Murray's the self-doubt all madly successful women carry around like an itch between their shoulder blades. He's Roger Clinton and Richard III. Or maybe he's the dirt you get under your fingernails from climbing your way to the top, proof you didn't start out there and maybe don't belong. Regardless, a brother like Murray makes a guy like me look good—husband-material good.

There are limits though, and Murray reached his earlier this morning with the phone call. I knew it was him because afterward Beth crossed the kitchen, bathrobe parted a hair too widely. She had that look on her face, like she'd just robbed a jewelry store and knew she'd get away with it.

"It's not happening, Beth."

She placed a hand over my mouth. "He's my brother."

Beth hasn't been back to Wellston in the nine years I've known her. So far as I know, she hasn't seen Murray in that time either.

"Fine," I said. "But this is huge. We're talking my-whole-weekend-shot-and-you-owe-me-a-new-set-of-clubs huge."

She smiled and silently exited the room, sashaying either out of thanks or to gloat.

"We're talking the nice Epon clubs," I shouted after her. "Driver and all!"

●　　●　　●

You'll find Murray on our website in Wellston High School's class of '94. Two arrests for narcotics possession, a few assault charges that got dropped down to misdemeanors and community service. One six-month stint in Southeastern Correctional for possession of stolen goods—a Harley softail he bought off a friend for the red-flag-inducing low price of seventy-eight dollars.

murray

Murray isn't wholly responsible, I'm told. When he was eighteen, there was a fight or other incident, and his brain got rattled, not enough to make him a vegetable, but enough to tear away little chunks of his inhibition. Beth has hinted about the circumstances but never answered my questions. She's suggested, in some way, it was her fault. When I ask her to elaborate, she always deflects.

"I'll explain some day," she says. "Just not now."

● ● ●

I take a left by the volunteer fire station with the VFW attached and pull up to the house Murray rents from an elderly pastor. This is the only place Murray's lived for more than a few months. When Murray works, he works as a substitute mailman. Even with his record, he finagled the gig out of a buddy he knew at the post office. But it's part-time and doesn't draw much cash. Murray's been evicted at least half a dozen times from other places. Still, he's going on four years here, and I suspect it's the pastor's abundant well of forgiveness. That or Murray supplies the old guy with weed.

The house is actually massive. Two-and-a-half stories with a cupola and wraparound porch. It's fallen into disrepair, graying paint on the wooden siding, shingles clipped away by wind, and one window knocked out and replaced with particle board. Livable only by squatter's standards.

I climb the stairs and press the doorbell. When I hear nothing, I knock.

"You looking for me?"

I turn around to see Murray standing in the oil-stained yard, his motorcycle boots up around his sun-grayed jeans. He's wearing a purple "Race for the Cure" T-shirt about a size too small and a cowboy hat with a brim that's been abused into two curls perched over each ear. A slight disruption in the hair on the left side of his head is all that hints at the scar, which I know slides up into his scalp. He usually has it hidden under a hat, his hair slicked back, but when he sweats it's visible, a pale pink that reminds you Murray is Murray. He's also sprouted a moustache since I last saw him, and he's wearing dark sunglasses that pinch his nose.

"Yes, Murray," I say. "I am looking for you." I'm set to deliver my speech, but Murray charges up the stairs, swings his arm around my shoulders, and whisks me into the house. I can't say whether or not I'm going of my own free will.

• • •

Inside is a wide hallway leading all the way to the back. The house used to be a funeral home. The bottom floor contains three large rooms—two to the left; one to the right—each with its own set of sliding double-doors. I think about what kind of awful day it must have been in the small town of Wellston, Ohio when they needed all three of those rooms at once. Some mining accident maybe. Three men on the same day. The mourners slipping between services. The heavy doors sliding on their runners like whispers in the wood.

Now though the house is dark and quietly stale. I get the impression there hasn't been electric on in a long time. In the front room is a shabby living space. A Coleman lantern rests on a stool next to a left-leaning recliner, which looks like it's been hauled out of a dumpster.

Walking toward the back of the house, Murray says, "You didn't tell Beth anything, did you?"

"What do you mean? You *talked* to Beth."

He presses a finger to his forehead. I smell sweat but no alcohol.

"Are you high?" I say.

He tilts his sunglasses down as if to show me the state of his eyes. The hallway is so dim his irises are nothing but dark little sockets. A wave of fear ripples through my stomach.

"Murray, what is this?"

He points deeper into the house. "Back here."

murray

He keeps his arm around me. We stride slowly, hip to hip. To my right the room is closed, but the oak doors have been warped from a leak in the ceiling. They no longer slide together properly. Through the crack I see that the floor of the room beyond is covered with stacks of small rectangular piles. Letters.

Thousands upon thousands, by my guess.

"Murray."

"Not there."

"Murray, what the hell?"

He turns to face me and holds my wrists. His breath— definitely not alcohol. Just the lingering smell of a break- fast burrito, which is so much more sinister.

"Look," he says. "I do these mail routes, right? Some- times I lighten the load. Just trash, okay? Circulars. Junk mail. People don't want that shit anyway. Saves everybody a hassle."

"Just junk mail," I repeat, like I'm a member of a cult.

"That's right. But I keep it all. Just in case. If somebody ever says—if they go, 'Murray, I don't get credit card offers anymore.'—then maybe I find their stuff and I throw in a couple."

"Has anyone ever said that?"

"No. Mostly the routes are rural. Mailboxes on the road. I drive my car. I don't talk to residents."

"You can still deliver the letters." I'm babbling. "All of it's in there?"

"I'm not worried about that."

"It's a federal offense, Murray." I can't get that phrase out of my head—federal offense federal offense—and now I'm talking in whispers, like the place is bugged. "That's prison, Murray. *Real* prison."

"I already did prison." He says it like it's a one-off thing, similar to mandatory military service in other countries.

"You could dole it out over several weeks, get rid of the out-of-date coupons. Burn them." I'm surprised at how quickly I'm considering the angles. Is that how criminals speak? 'Angles'? "No evidence, no crime," I say. "They can't make anything stick." I'm drumming up every line from every syndicated crime thriller I've ever half-watched on TNT.

Murray shakes his head. He slips the sunglasses back over his eyes. In the lenses, I'm a weak reflection of myself.

"That's not why I called," he says. He ushers me back to the last room and slides back the door to reveal a single, very short pile of letters. The small stack sits in the center of a bare floor. It's like an art installation. The blinds are all drawn, and thin slats of light rake the floorboards.

"Sometimes I get lonely," he says. He sits on the floor and holds his hands over the stack like he's warming himself over the embers of a campfire.

"It's here I got my problem," he says.

It's hard to distinguish details, but one thing's clear. Every one of these letters—about two or three dozen—has been opened. They're all stacked, their frayed ends to the right so they lean to the left like the recliner in the front room.

I'm moaning. I can hear myself as I step forward. The words escape me in whimpering and girlish syllables.

"What did you do, Murray? God damn it, what did you do?"

"I ain't never asked for help before. You know that. But I'm asking it now."

It's a ridiculous statement. Murray's begged money a thousand times, finagled assistance from friends and relatives his whole life. But none of that matters now. I think of Beth.

"What kind of help do you need?" I say. "If it's something illegal—"

He waves me off. "I need you to drive me somewhere. I need you to help me smooth things over. It's a girl."

"What girl?"

He slaps his knees and rubs his thighs without looking up. He's just staring at the letters.

"Murray, what girl?"

murray

He looks up, and his usual half-grin is gone. All I can see is the smooth whites of his cheeks below his sunglasses.

"I'm in love, Tom. We're in love."

●　●　●

Murray insists I read at least a few of the letters.

"So you understand," he says.

They're from a woman named Maria Vasquez and they're addressed to her grandmother, also named Maria. It's the normal stuff, asking about the older woman's welfare, the state of her house, and after other members of the far-flung family. What's immediately evident, however, is the woman's gift for language. While her questions to the elder Maria verge on the mundane, her descriptions of her own life—her updates about days spent in the shade of her backyard, amid friends at church functions, in movie theaters, or on errands—flow like rivers of cool water across murmuring stones.

The younger Maria's letters seem to be a freeing exercise for her creative spirit. Gold nasturtiums pucker at the pale moon; in one trip to a local beauty pageant, she describes the glistering lips of dolled-up little girls as slow salamanders floating in the spotlight. But most of all there is the tenderness. Her expressions of devotion to her nana are sleek and affectionate declarations not to be boasted by the most heart-sick young poet for his absent lover. I feel Maria Vasquez's care, her undying warmth, pouring from every page. It's familial but it captures something more—the feel of old heart pangs conjured from deeply felt memories. It makes me long for all the quiet moments of intimacy I've ever shared with loved ones.

I hand a letter to Murray. "What am I supposed to get out of this?"

"You don't feel it? It's poetry, man. She's genuine."

The thought of Murray plumbing the same depths, imbibing on the same sense of infinite beauty, disturbs me. We're not the same, he and I. Murray is all base desire, drug

177

addictions, cons, a broken parade of chain-smoking lovers and back-alley affiliations.

"So what if it's poetry?" I say. "You stole this woman's letters. What the hell were you thinking?"

"I was thinking, I'm in love."

"That is not—what? Why would you even say that?"

"It's not like I do it to everybody, man. It's not like I'm opening all the mail of everybody on my route. That'd be ridiculous. I saw her, okay. She's beautiful. You can't believe how beautiful. And then with the letters, you know, she's beautiful on the inside, too."

"Whatever it is, Murray, whatever you've done—you need to work it out."

"You have to help me," he says. "You have to vouch for me."

"Why would I do that?"

"We started writing each other."

That moan escapes me again.

"Is it her husband, Murray? Is that it? Is this a jealous boyfriend? Did you fight this guy, smash out his windows?"

"Nothing like that."

"Murray, are we talking police involvement? Just tell me."

"It's her dad," he says, "I need you to talk to her dad." He idly opens one of Maria's envelopes and sniffs it.

And right there the world stops. Right there—without Murray saying another word—it hits me. I hold out my arm like a crossing guard, which is the only thing I can think to do because my voice has died in my throat. I stare at Murray with what I hope is a pleading expression; it might be closer to the way I'd look melting on the surface of the sun.

"Yeah," he says. "You caught me. She's fifteen."

• • •

Beth finally answers the fourth time I call.

"What is it, Tom? I'm working."

"Did he tell you what this was about?"

"He didn't. He doesn't tell me anything."

"This is criminal, Beth."

"He's my brother."

"I don't care he's your brother. He's in love with a fifteen-year-old girl. They're pen pals."

She hesitates. There's that pregnant hum burrowing into the silence. Finally she mutters an "Oh Jesus" away from the phone.

"Is this about what happened?" I say. "In his past? Is there something to this? Is Murray some kind of"—I lower my voice—"you know, pedophile?"

"Stop it," she says.

"Tell me otherwise, Beth. Say it straight out."

"I'm sure it's not that," she says.

"He stole her mail. Somewhere there's a little old lady out there wondering why her granddaughter never writes. That's federal, Beth."

"He has problems. It's nothing as bad as you say. I just need you to do this for me, Tom. He can't take another strike. You know that better than anybody."

"This goes way beyond golf clubs."

"Do whatever he needs you to do."

"Simple as that, huh?"

"Simple as that. Do it for me," she says. "It's important. Last time I'll ask."

"You're too good," I say. "You're like an angel."

"I'm not," she says, and hangs up.

• • •

We're driving up 327 into a patch of backwoods where the sunlight's gone gray. The hills churn up further and further into more and more remote tangles of trees until we're passing an old logging lane and turning off onto a gravel side road.

Murray sits beside me tapping his thigh. He's still wearing the sunglasses despite the deep shade from the trees.

"I love her, man," he says. "You understand that, right? You got Beth, man. You love Beth. So you understand." He turns toward me. His arm is propped on the dash and he leans against the door. He's not wearing his seatbelt, and I think I might be able to shoot my arm past him, pull the handle, and kick him into the ditch.

"Beth," I say, "has the good sense to stay away from you. Beth—I don't want you bringing her into it."

"Course I'm bringing Beth into it. You guys have something special. You should know *special* when you see it. If anybody should understand, it's you."

He lights a cigarette, and I don't stop him. I'm picking my battles.

"And Beth," he says, "for your information, stays away because she knows what she did." He takes off his cowboy hat and pushes his hair off his forehead. He scratches at the pink scar, irritated and standing out now, jagged over his left ear.

"What do you mean, '*what she did*,' Murray?"

"Nothing, man."

"Beth," I say, "isn't fifteen. Beth and I were adults when we met. We're adults now. *You're* an adult now."

"Don't matter. You woulda known, man. That's my point. If you met Beth—she was fifteen and you were eighty?—wouldn't matter. You'd know. Soul mates."

Murray, for all his idiocy, assumes Beth and I are cosmically bonded. Corny as it sounds, Beth, for her part, has never given me reason to doubt it. But me—I've always assumed I tricked her into loving me. I'm always waiting for the corrections to come in the mail, for Beth to one day hop out of bed, skip downstairs, and never return.

"God damn it, Murray. You swear to God you haven't done anything with this girl? Nothing illegal?"

"Except the mail stuff?"

"The letters, yes. Other than stealing her mail"—federal offense federal offense—"you promise, you haven't—"

"Dinged her?"

"Had sex, anything like that? Anything *remotely* like that?"

"I promise, T. I'd wait forever for this girl."

180

I slow the car as the road turns into an endless series of washed out ruts. "I absolutely cannot believe I'm a part of this, right now."

"Kin, man. I'd do the same for you." He points. "It's up here, T."

To the right a gravel drive leads up a hill to a rustic cabin. I stop the car at the bottom of the drive. The whole lawn is all grown up and natural. It looks like that hill at the beginning of *Little House on the Prairie*. I half expect Maria Vasquez to come bounding down in a bonnet.

"What now?" I say.

"I just need you to be like a character witness."

"You've talked to this man?"

"Maria talked to him. He's home tonight."

• • •

It's getting on toward evening, and there's a cast iron knocker on the door in the shape of a fist. I'm trying to draw conclusions about this man who I'm supposed to—what am I supposed to tell this guy? What can a guy with a fifteen-year-old daughter be thinking when another man, twenty years older than his daughter, shows up with yet another guy to help 'explain the situation,' as Murray puts it? What can the *father* be thinking? I know what I'd be thinking, and its articulation might involve a firearm.

Murray pulls the knocker and drops it so it makes a loud *clunk* on the door. The door opens immediately.

The guy has to be seven feet tall. His forehead is hidden by the top of the doorway. I take a step back. He looks Latino with wide, high cheekbones and a jaw like a brick. He's as wide as Murray and me put together. Behind him, what little I can see of the room looks cozy, bright with a low fire in the fireplace. Books line the thick oak shelves built into the wall. There's a dark leather chair in the corner.

"I've been expecting you," he says.

Murray nods like, yes, yes, we're here to talk business. We step inside.

"I'm Murray," Murray says.

"Tomas," says the man.

I mumble my name—"Tom"—as I slide past him.

"Tom and Tom," says Murray, slapping his thigh, as if this puts us all on even ground.

"I doubt we're named for the same person," Tomas says. He leads us back through a pristine, granite-tiled kitchen with a massive island and a cooking range. All is simultaneously airy and rustic and immaculate. There's no sign of the girl. We walk out onto the back patio, where a fire pit has been cut out of the middle of the decking. A few steaks are sizzling on a low-lying grill over a cast iron pot of burning applewood. Tomas immediately flips the steaks, and for the first time, after getting past the size of him, I notice he's wearing a neat white apron. Murray and I must have interrupted the grilling process. I hope, on top of everything else, we aren't responsible for ruining his steaks.

"Where's Maria?" Murray says.

Tomas doesn't stop, per se, but there's a ripple in the enormous muscles of that broad back. It's a split second quiver like a horse flinching under a fly bite.

"She won't be joining us."

"Where is she?"

"I wanted us to talk this out, like men." He fusses over the steaks with a pair of tongs.

"I don't know about that, man," Murray says.

That whole back-muscle thing again.

"Come on, Murray," I say. "Let's not start off on a bad note."

Murray takes the hint only when I grip his forearm. I motion for him to sit down in one of the deep Adirondack chairs.

"Pour yourself a drink," Tomas says.

I obey, retrieving three tumblers. At Murray's request and Tomas's assent, I provide us all with Johnny Walker Black Label.

"Too bad you ain't got the blue label," Murray says. "I

ain't never tried that." He puts his feet up on a little wood-en ottoman. His biker boots jingle as the chains around his ankles settle.

"I have the blue label," Tomas says without adding more.

"Maria says you were some kind of football star."

Again the flinch. Tomas draws in his huge right arm al-most involuntarily.

"I played for the Oilers," he says.

"Is that still a team?"

"No."

"Austin?"

"Houston," Tomas says.

"Warren Moon," I say, trying to placate.

"I played offensive tackle," Tomas says. "I protected War-ren for seven years. I'm a man used to protecting."

For want of something to add, I say, "That's interesting."

Tomas doles out the steaks, puts them on sturdy green plates, rustically thick and textured. There's nothing else. Nothing but the steak and the whiskey. He hands us each two knives, no forks. We sit around the fire chewing like cavemen.

Murray and Tomas stare at one another. I wait for some-thing to begin, but the steak is thick. After a while the si-lence gets to me. I finally say, "What can we do to make this right?"

Tomas looks at me like I just arrived. A wad of steak is tucked into his right cheek. He finishes it off slowly and swallows.

"You can leave my daughter alone," he says. "You can leave her alone now, and I won't press charges. Then I can promise to kill either of you if I ever see you again."

I'm trying to be calm, to ignore the threat. I turn to Mur-ray. "He's right. You have to stop seeing her. That's fair, Murray."

Murray sets down the two knives, picks up the steak with his fingers. He takes a bite of the steak the way a hyena tears into a zebra's haunch. The dark, thin blood rolls down the side of his hand. He swallows hard because the piece is way too big. "I tell you what, Tom, how about you tell this big son-of-a-bitch I'll wait till she's eighteen, or he comes around and signs them papers to get married when she's sixteen. I ain't giving up. Not on love. She's a poet, and she's touched my soul."

"I think he can hear you, Murray."

"Not even if it means I got to fight to the death."

Murray lets the steak drop to the patio. It makes a fleshy smack on the treated wood. He sets down his plate and scoops up the steak knives.

Everything slows down now. There's a fire dying in the house. There's a fire dying here in front of us. The sun is tilting away into the hill. The low stir of our breathing is suddenly alive with possibility. The next move is what defines us.

"Don't let this get out of hand, Murray."

"You read the letters, Tom."

"They aren't worth dying over."

"Love is always worth dying over."

Tomas is a mountain in the dusk.

"You're talking stupid," I say.

"Am I? You know what you got?" Murray turns toward me.

"What?"

"You got Beth. She's a goddamn one-and-only."

There's a fevered look in his eye when Murray says this, and I'll know what it means someday. A long time from this moment—ten or fifteen years—I'll make Beth tell me. I'll sit her down after getting back from a high school basketball game where our daughter, Claire, just scored twenty-one points and nabbed seven rebounds. There'll have been a brief pow-wow after the game in which Claire negotiated a night out with friends and a subsequent sleepover.

We'll be alone, Beth and I, in the house. Beth, for some unknown reason, will look wistful and jumpy all at once. She'll be biting her nails and standing, then sitting, and

184

standing again. I'll beg her to tell me what's on her mind, insisting in that way I do. But, as with all things, it'll be Beth, really, who decides when the timing is right.

"Murray," she'll say. "Claire being out tonight makes me think of Murray."

By then I'll have my own reconfigured associations with Murray.

"Things changed between us when we were teenagers," she'll say. "I was in high school, and we'd always been close, but things changed." Then she'll let loose in what seems like a long, single breath everything she's been holding onto since before we ever met.

• • •

Beth's story will be about a girl. Thirty years before. Sixteen, with dark brown hair cut short, her acid-wash jeans tight and showing off all she's got, which is a lot. The girl has on a yellow T-shirt with a screen-print logo—a local pizza joint. It's hot for this far into September, and the band is still playing over the hill in a post-football-game salute that rises up out of the high school stadium along with the white lights blotting out a portion of the stars.

She's walking the tracks because it's a shorter way home to a trailer park near the fire station, same one with the VFW attached and the elderly men smoking on Monday nights. But this evening everyone is at the game, just leaving it in whoops and whistles. The Rockets have won, and the cars not far off, on the main drag, are separated from this girl by a spindly barrier of trees, a mucky brook full of Mountain Dew cans and cigarette butts and old milk cartons, and near that are a couple rust-mottled sheds tagged in graffiti of the simplest type, the kind of amateur missives that look like cave drawings compared to stuff in cities. A blotchy blue scrawl announces that Eddie loves Wanda like crazy.

The tracks are quiet. Though the sounds from Main Street are only a hundred feet away, somehow the barrier of trees makes her path along the tracks an untouchable thing.

Three young men are only fifty yards away. They haven't seen her yet, but they will. The three of them passed a rickety farm about two miles back as they walked into town, and two of them killed a couple baby rabbits in their hutch just to see what it felt like. They broke the rabbits' necks by twisting their heads. The third boy didn't participate, but he watched and didn't say a word. He smoked a cigarette and put it out under his boot near the place where one of the boys threw a rabbit down. The third boy walked away after that, and it's the only thing that kept the other two from killing the remaining rabbits where they slept.

The two killers are red-faced, bleach-eyed, freckled from near three weeks under the sun working to frame up a barn. They've been paid under the table each Friday, and on the third Friday—tonight—they left for good with dreams of sex and a little pot if they could get it. They are told there's a party in a field outside town after the game, and there will be girls there, high school kids only a little younger than themselves. They'll see about buying beer in the Main Express convenience store, and if not, see about stealing a few cans in a baggy jacket one boy has tied about his waist.

They see the girl at the moment she sees them, and one boy chuckles. He has killed a rabbit and now is chuckling at a single girl on the train tracks with her arms crossed under her breasts, and her breasts prominent in a thin yellow T-shirt.

To say the boy thinks of rape would be to oversimplify. He thinks only of convincing the girl to fool around with him in the woods. He thinks of convincing her to unbutton his pants and to do things with her mouth. He asks if she likes beer.

She says she's headed home.

The boy who did not kill a rabbit stands back in the dark, not moving forward like the other two, not talking.

When the girl tries to push past, the two rabbit-killers

186

throw her to the ground. There's a sound of tearing cotton and the scree of the railbed shifting under boots and
hands. That's when the third boy grows a strength in him.
A strength he didn't have with the rabbits but wishes he
had. He picks up a rock from the creek bed. It's a jagged
stone the weight of a book maybe, and it's awkwardly angled and ill-held. He steps behind the other two boys, who
have pinned the girl to the ground. He slams the stone
into their ribs. He clubs them between the shoulders and
neck. A deep gash makes blood run out a hole in one boy's
shirt.

The third boy gets in a few more blows before one of the
other two swings something at him and strikes him in the
head. He shudders but keeps pounding them with the rock
until they flee.

Now the third boy is standing alone with the rock still
in his hand. He stares at the girl with her shirt torn all the
way down to her navel, her bra broken. She's indecent because she isn't even thinking to cover herself. She's trying
to re-fasten the button on her jeans, but it's not there. The
button has flown off into the woods, and the boy thinks
he might come back and look for it later in the daylight in
case she can sew it back on. For now though the girl is indecent in the spill of stadium light working through the trees.
He can see her breasts. They're whiter than he remembers
from years ago when she was still unashamed to show him
her body. It's hard for him to think of her as his sister right
now.

"I love you," he says, and he has no idea what he means
by it.

In the scuffle, one of the other boys has struck him with
something, maybe a piece of iron from the railbed. Whatever it was, it made a long cut in the boy's skull above his
ear. He's shivering now, looking at this woman/girl, who is
his sister and not his sister in his brain. The sight of her is
exciting and familiar and, he thinks, my wires are a little
crossed. His hand shakes so bad he drops the rock.

"I love you," he says again. Again he has no idea what he means by it.

Sitting in our living room, after our daughter's game, Beth will say it. She'll say, "Murray just got stuck. It was like he never gave up on loving a young girl he wasn't allowed to have. He never gave up trying to make it right."

And though I'll mumble something without weight, I'll understand Maria Vasquez a little better. I'll understand in a vague way how a mind can get put on pause, how love can grow twisted and unassured so that a young girl, even one who is your sister, saved in a moment of danger, can become all a man understands, the object of all purpose. The notion is muddled and perverse, but I'll sense it, the way Murray's mind came to be, his obsession with Beth, but not the real Beth. Then I'll think of our daughter Claire and how I could snap the neck of a man, any adult man, who tried to take her away.

"I failed Murray," Beth says, "because I didn't know how to take care of him after that. His mind wasn't right. He needed my help, but I've never been able to go back."

●　●　●

Murray lurches forward with a steak knife gripped in either hand. The blades are pointed down, and he raises his arms over his head. He leaps past the fire pit at Tomas Vasquez, and I have to believe, even to this day, in order to live with myself, that his full intention was only to scare Tomas, not to stab him or kill him.

I'd like to believe it was only a show, but I'll never know. Because there are rare moments when certain things—things you've possessed a hazy knowledge of your entire life—suddenly zip their way into glaring perspective. They happen so quickly, so abruptly, that they make you realize you've never really understood anything. In this case, the speed and strength with which Tomas Vasquez reacted made it clear I'd never fully comprehended professional athletes. Not really. Not how much more impressive, even well into their post-playing days, they are than the rest of us.

Tomas tucks in his right arm the way he did when he was cooking steaks. In the years to come, I'll watch his old games on an on-demand NFL Classic station. He does the same thing. Tucks that arm in tight, his palm flat, the left arm held out like a feeler to catch a defensive end or linebacker. And just at the moment the pass rusher—the howling, massive, leg-pumping brute charging the quarterback—reaches him, Vasquez releases that thirty-six-inch-thick right arm like a spring. You always see the jolt as his punch hits home, even in the big men, the sudden shudder of their shoulder pads, the momentary flap like a beetle's wings as the strike connects, the way the other man's step hitches, the cleat swiping at the grass in a wasted motion. Vasquez is near three hundred pounds, all muscle, and sometimes he bends them backwards to the ground in one liquid movement.

On the patio, with Murray leaping toward him, Tomas shoots that arm up and hits Murray just between the sternum and windpipe, a place in the upper rib just over Murray's heart. The blow makes a blunt meaty thump as visceral as Murray's steak hitting the patio. There's a cracking sound. Flesh and bone. The knives are gone immediately. They fly from Murray's hands as if they've been yanked away on strings. Murray cartwheels, mid-air, over the deck chair, arms flailed, landing like a tossed doll.

Tomas Vasquez rises to his feet.

I step in front of him.

"Don't do it, boss," I say. "He's down."

For a moment I think he's going to hit me. I know he's thinking about it.

"How do we make this right?" I say.

"I should call the police."

"This'll blow over," I say. "I'll make it blow over." I can think of nothing else but to pull out my checkbook and write out a check for ten thousand dollars. I've had a good year. I don't know why I do it. I should let Vasquez finish Murray off. I should at least let him call the police. If Murray's crazy enough to attack the man with steak knives, who knows what he'll do? I wonder briefly if I'm facilitating a far more serious crime yet to occur.

But something, maybe it's the way Murray's eyes told me something about Beth, about the two of them, or maybe it's that scar that shines a bloodless pink through the matted hair where his hat has been knocked off. But I'm doing my best to save Murray now. Maybe it's not the most noble gesture. I am, after all, a guy throwing money at a problem, the way rich men have done from the beginning of time. But it's all I have at the moment.

Vasquez looks at the check, then tucks it into his pocket.

"Leave," he says. "Don't come back. Or I'll kill him. And I'll have every right."

I help Murray up. He's doubled over. His clavicle is broken. His left arm, which lies limp, turns inward at an odd angle. He winces with every step and breathes strangely.

"We need to get you to a hospital," I say. I lead him out of Vasquez's home. It's over, just like that. Murray moans as I put him in the passenger seat. I wonder if I would have been doing him a favor by pushing him out of the car before we arrived.

II

That night, I took Murray to the hospital and told a nurse he'd fallen awkwardly against a curb. It seemed plausible enough, and they didn't ask other questions. Murray went along with it. I left before the examination was up. He looked like an old dog lying there on the stretcher. An old dog waiting to be put down.

I didn't see him for five or six years. A few months before I saw him, I'd read that Maria Vasquez had won an award, something national and prestigious for her poetry, which she'd collected already, as a junior in college, into a book that was to be published by a major press the following year. There was some hullabaloo about this. There were claims she'd plagiarized. Articles citing other young people who notoriously stole from earlier writers for the purpose of fame, but no one came forward with proof about Maria. I'd followed the story for a few weeks, and then it passed out of my consciousness. Seeing Murray suddenly at my doorstep one evening, I wondered briefly if Maria's fame were related to his visit. I wondered if he would ask me about her. He didn't.

He'd lost weight. His moustache had gone gray. He'd been working as a roofer on condos somewhere near Wilmington. It struck me that Claire was, by then, four years old, and Murray had never seen her. I thought about asking him if he wanted to meet his niece, but I realized I didn't want him to. Murray, in his newly broken and hangdog visage, only asked for Beth. I let him in.

Beth hadn't yet told me about the two of them as teenagers and what happened on the railroad tracks, or I may have stayed. Instead, I took a walk to give them privacy. I got eaten by mosquitoes, and by the time I returned, scratching at my forearms, Murray had gone. Beth was standing on our porch looking out at the thick loblolly pines surrounding our house. I could barely see her face in the dark.

"He ask for money?" I said.

She shook her head. "Don't be an asshole. He's broken."

"Broken or broke?"

"It's not like that. He was saying goodbye."

"He going to join the army?"

"I said don't be an asshole. He's my brother."

"You sure don't act like it," I said. Beth and I had been having money troubles. A few startup ventures I'd invested in were doing poorly, and they were threatening a plan I had to retire in ten years. I'd never let go of the fact that Beth was too good for me, and financial disappointments, even slight ones, were setting me off on long bouts of self-pity that kept her at bay. I was being surly as a result.

"He's going to Alaska, if you have to know. A friend of his got him work in a warehouse on the north slope, something to do with maintenance on the pipelines. I don't know. He just said he was going and he probably wouldn't be back."

"Ever? We'll never see him again?" I cracked a smile. Something about my pay-off to Tomas Vasquez had kept me tethered to Murray. I'd been saddled for years with the thought that I was one day going to get a visit from police officers telling me there'd been a murder, and why had I paid Tomas Vasquez such an exorbitant sum? Either that, or Murray would be asking me for more cash, either for Vasquez or some other father, or maybe he was on the lam, needed getaway money. These scenarios had all crossed my mind again when I saw him this evening. But the look on his face had thrown me off just enough. Murray hadn't looked like he wanted anything, just to see Beth, like he said.

"Just don't be an asshole," Beth said again.

I didn't respond. Somehow Murray going to Alaska felt just far enough away to put all my fears at ease.

"I know," I said to Beth. "He's your brother. I get it."

We didn't sleep in the same room for weeks after that.

• • •

Almost exactly a year after Murray showed up at my door, I receive an envelope. Inside is a computer print-out of one of the articles about Maria I've already read.

There's also a second print-out. I recognize it as a page from my own website. Our folks in design created a template that looks like a folder on a detective's desk, complete with coffee-stain rings in the lower right hand corner and some hand-written remarks. The name on the page is 'Tomas Vasquez.'

Claire, five now, clomps into the room looking bored, the way she does whenever Beth and I are working in different rooms of the house.

"What's this?" she says. She picks up the envelope.

"I'm trying to figure that out, hon."

She turns over the envelope and I see in the upper left-hand corner Tomas's name above a return address in Ohio. I search the envelope again and find a tiny slip of paper that says, *Please come. In person.*

And maybe because I'm curious, or guilty, or simply afraid, I obey. The next day I travel to Wellston, Ohio for the first time since I left Murray at the hospital.

I use the old knocker in the shape of a fist, and Tomas answers the door again. In some ways I'm expecting him to be lessened by the intervening years, diminished, the way Murray was, but he's robust as ever. He's maybe wider in the mid-section, girthier, but it only adds to his magnificence.

"Come in," he says.

This time we sit before the unlit fireplace in his den. It's a peaceful room glowing gold with the amber light bouncing off the wood of the book cases. We sit in two leather chairs across from one another. Again he offers me a drink.

"No," I say. "I came to find out why you sent me this." I hold up the print-out with his information.

"I thought you might not have seen it."

"You'd be right."

"Part of me thought you'd have looked me up after that night."

"I didn't want to have anything to do with you. You did a good job scaring both of us off."

"I did," he agrees, "but now I want you to know."

I nod, but I don't fully understand. "So you're wanting to explain this? Is that it?" I read his charges off the sheet. "Felony domestic violence. Aggravated assault. One month in FDC Houston."

"It should have been three to five years," he says. "I was playing then. Making the most money of my career. The charges were in the off-season, and the judge was a big football fan. He locked me up for the summer. I was back in time for training camp, no fines from the NFL."

"I still don't get it."

"It was Maria's mother. Maria, of course, wasn't born then, but we were together a long while before we had her."

"And you fought?"

He smiles. "Fighting would imply it was an even match." He looked at his empty hand as if not pouring the drink had left some hole in how he'd seen this conversation going. "All I can say is I was an angry man. I got off on hurting people. The game makes you that way."

"Sounds like an excuse," I say.

"You're right, of course. We weren't particularly poor growing up. I didn't even have that chip on my shoulder. Not like my mother's people who came up from Michoacán. They tapped pine resin for a turpentine manufacturer. Tough work. They had nothing. Me, I had it easy compared to them."

"What's this have to do with me?"

"You're in a position to see all sides," he says. "Or maybe it's because I took your money. Maybe I think that buys you an explanation."

"What if I don't want one?"

"You ever hear of a devil's bargain? Maybe your money buys you an explanation, whether you want it or not."

"I'll take that drink, then."

He smiles slightly. He pours us Johnnie Walker Blue Label, neat.

"You remembered," I say.

"Maybe your friend Murray deserves this more," he says. "That's what I want to say."

"Why?"

"He could see me for what I was."

I take a drink of the whiskey and wait out the silence. Tomas begins.

"The first time Murray came to the house, I'd been chopping wood and, on my way into the garage, I dropped the axe. It came down on my calf, took a little chunk of flesh. Nothing major, but I was bleeding like a stuck pig. Made me angry. I felt the old heat come back into my chest.

I ranted, just howling and swearing, throwing tools, breaking a few pieces of antique furniture. It'd been a while since I'd been that violent, but I let loose. Soon as I was finished, I walked out into the drive—panting—and there's Murray standing on my porch chewing on a goddamn toothpick with a package in his hand. I hadn't heard him pull up. Cool as anything, he says, 'I need you to sign for this.'"

Tomas smiles fully. "That brother-in-law of yours has one shit-eating grin."

I raise my tumbler to that.

"You should know," he says, "he didn't start writing her letters until after that. He'd been stealing hers, yes, but we racked that up to terrible service. We even made a few complaints. All I'm saying is that he didn't write to her until after that day with the axe. I think, after seeing me and my anger, he was checking up on her. I pieced this together after you guys showed up here. I made Maria tell me everything. She, of course, didn't know about my temper tantrum in the garage, but when she gave me a look at the letters, they were dated. I did the math myself."

"What did his letters say?"

"They ask after her. They also cross a line, yes. Declarations of love. But they aren't explicit. I see that now." He holds up a sheaf of trifolded letters. They've been sitting all this time on a small table beside his chair. "They're not predatory, I suppose."

He stands with the letters as if he's going to walk them to me, lay them in my lap. Then he leans down and sets them in the fireplace. He opens a large antique tinder box on the mantle and produces a fireplace match.

"Given distance and a little time," he says, "I might even have appreciated what your brother-in-law had to say." He lights the match.

"What are you doing?"

"I'm protecting my daughter."

"Like you did before," I say.

"Not like before. One of the things you might be asking yourself is, Why tell you this after seven years?"

"I guess you're going to get to that." I'm talking quickly, trying to get to the part where we discuss whether the lit match hovering over Murray's old letters is a good thing. A big part of me knows that right there is maybe the last evidence of any crime Murray may have committed. And it's about to go up in flame. This should thrill me. Considered alongside Murray's removal to Alaska, I should be ecstatic. But that's not how these things work: relief is never whole. I'm dying to read them now, the letters. I'm dying to know why Tomas kept them so long. Is there some explanation that lends sense to what my money and time and worry, and even Beth—her undying commitment—mean?

"My wife left me pretty soon after Maria was born. I was still a very angry man then. I thought it might help, moving here, somewhere remote. I picked it at random. A friend of mine hunted deer every year not far from here, and I came out with him once. When Maria's mother left me, I remembered how far away this place felt from everything. I'd saved enough to retire on, live modestly, and still pay the alimony and child support.

"But a year after she left me, Maria's mother was dead. Inflammatory breast cancer. Bones, lymph nodes, lungs, all within a few months." He waved this off as searching for meaning amid flies. The lit match wavered. "Maria was my second chance. I raised her right. I re-built myself into something serene. I became love."

"I appreciate that," I say. I think of Claire, of my own failings and the ways I try to be a father. "But how does that explain why I'm here?"

"Maria's letters to her grandmother were what connected her to her mother. She started writing as a way—I don't know—to reach beyond this place. Your brother-in-law stole that from her."

The match goes out. He looks at it as if the plume of smoke is an especially good piece of magic.

murray

I stand up and approach the fireplace to try and casually lift the letters out of harm's way, but Tomas holds out his left arm, and—because I've seen the tapes by now; because I've seen what he did to Murray—I know the right hand can follow with a vengeance.

"You're not going to see these," he says. He lights another match, this time pausing only long enough to say, "I asked you here *now* because my daughter's book finally came out. She sent me a copy a couple weeks ago. I recognized a great many of the lines immediately, from these letters." He drops the match on the pages, and they grow into a pile of flame folding in on itself. "I have to protect my daughter," he says. "You don't strike me as a litigious sort of man, but still I can't let you see what he wrote. On the other hand, I at least needed you to know he wasn't as bad as you might have thought."

And right there I know those letters are not only the last vestige of evidence tying Murray to a few crimes, they're the last thread linking him to Maria and her work.

"And if you try and tell anyone," Tomas says, "about what I've told you, I'll deny every bit of it."

Then he does the most unexpected thing yet. He rises. And with the pages of Murray's old letters still burning in the fireplace, he hands me a copy of Maria's book.

"So you understand," he says. "I forgive your brother-in-law. I even forgive myself."

• • •

Someday, in the quiet house, an hour or so after Beth tells me the story of walking along the train tracks and about Murray coming to her rescue, about him suffering his injury, and after I finish fumbling with questions that have no answers, I'll finally put all the pieces together. I'll take down Maria's book from the shelf and I'll read Beth a particular poem. By then there'll have been what people like to call a 'following.' Poetry doesn't account for much today, I know, in the grand marketing scheme of things, but there'll be something people respond to, that strikes a chord, and Maria will be interviewed on national morning shows and afternoon programs alongside celebrities. She'll have a quiet way about her that speaks volumes. It'll eventually strike me that I've never seen her except on television.

The poem of Maria's I'll read Beth that evening is about a blind man who has his sight miraculously restored. The miracle turns out to be an awful thing. The blind man weeps night after night. When finally his wife questions him, he explains that most of us can't get past the way we see ourselves; we can't imagine how amazing and beautiful and good we look to those who truly adore us. We can't understand we're better people than we'll ever know. By being able to see his own image in mirrors and windows and lakes, the blind man has lost the only version of himself that ever mattered, the one through his wife's eyes which had stood in for his own.

I'll try, fumblingly, to tell Beth that this pertains to her. That if she could only see herself like I see her, she'd understand all she's done for Murray. I'll add something less than insightful like, "So try not to beat yourself up about it."

This will bring on her first smile since we got home from the basketball game. She'll say, "Tom, I think what you're not seeing is that the poem pertains to you. I've never had trouble understanding myself as being loved."

She'll leave it at that.

• • •

Somewhere in Alaska near the north slope is a corrugated steel building that houses equipment for oil rigs. Wind gathers the snow here along the dark blue outer wall in sheer white angles. Inside there's a man operating a forklift. He drinks some on especially cold nights, and he's known as a bit of a carouser. Yet there's something defeated about him. Maybe it's the scar running down through his thinning hair, or his tobacco-stained moustache or the pale, sunken cheeks that remind you he was once livelier and fuller-faced.

Maybe nobody really knows who he is. He has the odd habit of traipsing out into the snow some nights just to stand there for hours with his arms outstretched, as if he could embrace the entire spotless horizon.

This hasn't been confirmed, mind you, but there's a rumor he only goes out far enough not to be heard. Maybe that's true, maybe not. But one thing's clear—you can picture this man in his navy parka, the fur-trimmed hood, his breath rising like exhaust erupting from a struggling piece of machinery. And if you were somehow an angel, invisible and light, floating in on the frozen air—if you so chose, if you were so inclined, and you descended low enough to hear this man at the center of all this ice—you'd make out the sound of him.

Howling. He's howling to the entire world for someone to love.

fifty

He's not that old, but the contoured seat takes a toll none-theless, stiffens him up into a motionless hunch. He's six-ty-seven and wishes he'd married his wife sooner by a de-cade, because that'd make it fifty years, not forty, coming up on Sunday. He wishes she'd have dragged his ass out of history junior year where he was doodling portraits of tiny, nude women across a map of Waterloo on page 297. That would have been nice. She would have planted a fire-cracker-kiss on him, something with tongue, her fine, small breasts pressed against him, and she would have hauled him down to the county courthouse.

He wishes she'd have come along a decade earlier and that way he'd have had just that much longer before the leaving.

He's stopped now at the dusty roadside rest along a grand stretch of Ohio highway. Miles back he emerged from the southern hills into the shapeless farmland, a dish-water sky, limpid wheat swaying like an ongoing revival on either side of the road, and it all felt like a deep breath, a

fifty

walloping mad intake of freedom after all that dark, all that forest.

He's standing, he figures, right where the first honeymoon snapshot took place, a hamburger stand off the main drag, a shack really, with a dirt parking lot and a fugue of motorcycle engines crashing up against the oaks surrounding the picnic tables as a cadre of vets clamored in and dismounted. She'd shouted to one of them then, the tallest one with the homemade tattoo of a barn owl stretched down that long bicep dangling out of the sleeveless jean jacket with the patches, red and black, skulled and lightning-ed and announcing the name of his motorcycle club, which Donald could not now remember. And the man, this bearded tall vet with his angry smile, tooth-blackened bite, obliged and called her ma'am, and she laughed.

I'm twenty-six, she said. I'm not a ma'am.

And the biker said, You're married, ain't you?

And she said, yes, she was, only a few hours now.

And the biker said then yes, she was a ma'am, and he could think of no better thing to be: My mom's a ma'am, ma'am.

And he took the picture and handed back the camera, and they all ate hotdogs in the burnished sunlight, the slightly brass-tasting wind carrying their words to places unknown, to towns they'd never visit.

He places the camera now on a tripod, sets the timer, the easy pace of its clicking steadily speeding up as he walks away. The shudder snicks just as he positions himself, about fifteen feet out, hands behind his back, the long low country behind him and the grass and the absent hamburger stand, blown away by time and change and changelessness too, because it's the same place, he's certain, he can feel the love still warming the ground beneath his feet, like it spilled there decades ago and left a permanent mark.

• • •

He cuts north as his son calls, and there's that insurmountable thing between them, as it always is, has been since Jason

201

was fourteen, maybe thirteen, though now it's refined by the airwaves or the decryption of audio particulates and satellite relay.

"Come on home, Dad," he says. "She wouldn't want you out on the road."

"You wouldn't know," he says.

"Dad, be serious. You shouldn't be driving—where are you now? Ohio? If she'd have known you were going to take off, she would have said something."

"How do you know where I am?"

"It's a commercial GPS, dad. I can track it. It was an extra. I have them on all the trucks in the fleet."

He hangs up and stops on the side of the road where there's more wheat and more telephone lines, handholding, the cables swaying as if connected arms of great, stark children in a row, just waiting—red rover red rover.

Using a screwdriver that he keeps tucked alongside the tire iron, he pries out the bulky GPS console from its custom mount on the dash. He drops the boxy little computer into a ditch, then pushes the mud over it with his shoe like he's frosting a cake. He steps on it, his entire weight pushing it into the earth until it's buried and clouded over by a thin slurry of fetid water and he can no longer make it out. For a moment, standing like that, on one foot, he resembles a wading crane, his stooped shoulders and tall, thin body highlighted by the clothes clinging to his arms and legs in the wind. A lonely old bird.

. . .

And then he's on to the old zoo that's a big zoo now. On that weeklong honeymoon trip they stopped and only had time to see the gazelles pacing impatiently in their habitats before they had to leave and satiate the desires brought on by his touching of her hand, the slightest rubbing of their knuckles together.

He calls the house from his cell phone and gets the machine, and he doesn't leave a message because there's no one there to hear it.

fifty

He meets a young man outside the chimpanzee cages, where the gazelles used to be, and asks him kindly if he'll take the picture. There are new gazelles in a new habitat now, in the section of the zoo with the African animals, the elephants and rhinoceroses snorting dust, their black eyes wet as fish souls, and he doesn't want a picture by the gazelles because here by the chimpanzee cages is where the old gazelles used to be. The ground is warm again, and it's important to him. He's mapped it out, and this is where they stood when the elderly woman with the green hat snapped their picture four decades ago.

The boy takes the photo and says, "I didn't know they still made film, I guess."

"A film camera," the man says proudly. He's heard they're making a comeback, that all the digital effects still can't turn the crisp clarity of computerized memories into warm blurs of humanness, that people still aren't fooled. Maybe there's something in the inconsistencies, the things lost forever because they were never captured, that makes film superior to the technology, to the gray device his son bought him, with the automatic lens that pops out when you turn it on.

The kid hands him back the camera, and the old man tries to say something about how the young don't have memories. They're upside down. Memories, for the young, are of the future, and that's what makes the young who they are.

"We're like two men," he says, "and one of us walks on the ceiling, the other on the floor."

The boy is moving away, but still says over his shoulder, "Which one am I?"

The man shouts after him, "You'll find out!"

• • •

The last place he goes is a small church with broken-toothed floorboards, and it's not where they were married because this place was old then, too. He's impressed that the structure held on this long, the doomed rafters given up hope over the pewless floor and pulpitless dais for anyone to ever come again and sing songs that sound like flame, like paeans of life itself given freely to the air, all that living and yearning and singing, because it escapes, has to, or else the world would be too productive, too set on itself, so there has to be this release, and these rafters have lost the joy of it but not the memory.

The two of them, he and she, had felt so full of themselves, so reckless and naughty. She used the word 'fuck,' which he had never heard her use before, and he was so incredibly turned on by that. He loped dumbly behind her, she walking backward down the aisle, a few pews still there on their sides, and she said she wanted him so badly, and that there was nothing wrong in it.

Don't be such a prude, she said.

It's a church.

And we're married. We're married forever.

And they made love standing up because he was afraid of iron nails and snagging on the planks and tetanus, and his legs, he thought, had never ached so much even when he ran the long distance races in high school and used to taste the saltiness of his sweat on his lips after the race as if that were his prize, the secret taste of himself on his lips; and now that taste was her taste there, the two of them burning and tasting and it all surrounded by the grayness of the dust and grayness of the still sunshine and the darkness of the trees beyond.

He sets up the tripod and takes his picture in the warm place where the pulpit used to be, where they used to be.

•   •   •

Virginia.

The house is a silent, airless monument to the calm, that pervasive sense of wellness held in the neatness of a housewares magazine resting on the island near the stovetop, the inimitable angle of a scrub-brush perched at the edge of the sink over a dirty plate that looks clean. There's the pur-ple-hued scent of a candle burning on the sideboard in the hallway, and in it the promise that life is somehow close.

He carries the developed pictures in a white paper sleeve in the pocket of his old corduroy sport coat, and he holds his hand over the envelope so that it's becoming perhaps too humid in his grip.

He steps into the living room with a long stride that's all bluster, and he smiles too, to add to the face of his confi-dence.

"Dad," says his son. "Dear God, Dad. It's been three days." His son has gone paunchy a little, a trait from his wife's side of the family, though she never adopted it herself, always kept herself fit, but a family of farmers with hardy souls, and he always feels bird-like, a rickety stork plodding and without substance. He feels this way about his son, that his son is more real than him, and that the paunch, while a negative perhaps, is still testament to his son's reality, his grounded nature.

"Dad, I thought—"

"I told you I'd be back in time. I slept in my car."

"After the GPS, I thought, you know—"

He touches his son on the shoulder and still hopes they'll become friends someday, the way they were when his son was twelve, though he's not so naive to deny the possibili-ties are slim.

He steps into the bedroom, and she's there, lying half-cov-ered by the sheet, which runs over her chest and beneath both arms so her hands are small birds nesting naked and quiet on her thighs.

She is flat beneath the sheet, and he imagines the new scars beneath her shirt, which is no longer the hospital gown but a T-shirt he bought for her from a football game he went to with two other men, colleagues, nearly a decade ago. The shirt says, *Winning is a Full Contact Sport,* and it meant something to them then, something frivolous and funny he can't now remember. It means something differ-

205

ent now because somehow it's accumulated the seriousness and the sanctity and the spirit of her living today. He thinks how silly that is, how the old church was sapped of its holiness, and now something very much like that original holiness has come to rest in a ridiculous shirt printed in China with a nothing-logo, a battle cry for a fake battlefield and for a warrior spirit with no real consequences. Somehow all that means something now in the short, calm body of his wife breathing in the room where he stands, a goofy stork, at the foot of her bed.

She opens her eyes, and he's still a bit hunched, a bit ashamed of leaving during the operation, and he sidles like a child to her right as she reaches for him.

Her voice is hoarse. "I'll be fine," she says. "They got it all, they think. They think it looks good."

He lays his fingers on her forearm. Taps once with his index finger as if this one half-second tap, a measure of her realness, can start it all up again, the music and laughter and touching and world-walloping screams echoing in every barbecue, car trip, snow-shoveling, lawn-mowing, afternoon, thrown silverware in a fight that almost ended it all at the end of the Reagan era, and the constantly weaving monotony of time and time and time.

"What are you thinking about?" she says.

"Everything. I'm thinking about everything."

"Well, stop it. I'm here. You're here." She gives him a wry look.

"Jason told you I left."

"He told me," she says. "Almost as soon as I woke up. But I don't hold it against you. Not the past couple days, either. Hospitals aren't really your thing."

"I told Jason I'd be back. I told him you wouldn't spend a night in this house alone. I kept my word, but I needed those days. I'm burned out." He smooths the bedspread beside her. "I'm still sorry about it, though. I feel awful."

"Like I said, you're here now."

"It's selfish. This long, and I'm still selfish."

fifty

"What did you do, or should I even ask? Don't tell me if there were strippers involved." Her lips edge back into an easy smile.

He touches the photos of himself without her in their honeymoon spots, all in his pocket. "There weren't strippers."

"Then again," she says, "if there were strippers, maybe you have their numbers. The doctor I spoke to mentioned fake breasts. I think I'm going to fulfill a lifelong dream and get something big enough to give me back problems."

"I don't think you understand how strippers work. They don't give out their numbers. And I think you're lovely. You're lovely no matter what."

"They tattoo on a nipple," she says. "Or take a piece from somewhere else."

She was telling him this because he'd refused to hear any of it before. And now he feels ashamed about that, too.

"So what were you doing if not getting your rocks off?"

"Don't be vulgar."

"Vulgar is sneaking out while your wife is under the knife." She gives him a comically arch look, caricatured.

"I was traveling," he says, and thinks about giving her the photos, but is ashamed of them, also. Why did he need to see himself there, his singular, balding self surrounded by memories, all the most tangential parts of those places incompatible with what could be captured on a digital drive or even on his precious emulsion? There was no film like that. And he thinks how they have so much time yet together, that these pictures are nothing, that maybe ten years down the line, on their fiftieth anniversary, they'll both be there together. New photos will replace the ones he has of himself, of this time when he was alone for a little while because she was somewhere facing death and he had to get his head right, to think of himself as a solitary figure. And after all that, all that contemplating, he couldn't think of it, couldn't comprehend the vision of himself in that place as a one, a stark unaccompanied body, and he'd decided no such man existed.

"I was staking out a trip," he says.

"For us?"

"The places we drove on our poor, little honeymoon."

She touches the shirt over the new shape of her chest. "That sounds lovely," she says.

"We go when you recover," he says. "There's not much there, I'll warn you."

"You're an idiot," she says.

"Why?"

"Because there's always something there. It's always there even if you can't see it."

notes

"Straw Man" was the winner of the 2013 *Mississippi Review* Prize and is published in *Mississippi Review* 41.1&2.

"Patience is a Fruit" was the winner of *Yemassee's* William Richey Short Fiction Contest and appears in *Yemassee Journal* 20.1 Winter/Fall 2013.

"A Different-Sized Us" was the winner of *Bear Deluxe Magazine's* Doug Fir Fiction Award; the story was published in *Bear Deluxe Magazine* 35 (2013) as "The Quiet Held the Crocuses."

"Bethesda" was the winner of *Jabberwock Review's* 2013 Nancy D. Hargrove Editor's Prize for Fiction and appears in the *Jabberwock Review* 34.1, Summer 2013 issue.

"Courier" won *New South's* Annual Writing Contest for 2013, and appears in *New South* 6.2 (2013).

"Their Own Resolution" won *Ardor Literary Magazine's* Annual Short Story Contest; it is published in Issue 3 (2013).

"Hear It" is published in the Fall 2013 issue of *Crossborder*.

"Fifty" won the 2013 Miriam Rodriguez Short Story Contest and appears in *Carve Magazine's* Summer 2013 Premium Edition.

"Take Care" won third place in *Baltimore Review's* Winter Contest; it appears in *The Baltimore Review* print issue of 2013.

"Butterscotch" appears in the March/April 2014 issue of *The Magazine of Fantasy & Science Fiction*.

"Murray" appears, in a slightly altered version, as "Declarations" in *Narrative Magazine*.

author

David Armstrong's stories have won the *Mississippi Review* Prize, Yemassee's William Richey Short Fiction Contest, the *New South* Writing Contest, and *Jabberwock Review's* Prize for Fiction, among other awards. His latest stories appear in *Narrative Magazine, The Magazine of Fantasy & Science Fiction, Best of Ohio Short Stories,* and elsewhere. His story collection drive/memory, won the 2013 Emergency Press International Book Contest. He was awarded a Black Mountain Institute PhD Fellowship in Creative Writing (Fiction) and served as fiction editor of *Witness* magazine before receiving his PhD from the University of Nevada, Las Vegas. A lecturer in creative writing and literature at Gonzaga University, he now lives in Spokane, Washington, with his wife, Melinda.

ABOUT THE TYPE

This book was set in ITC New Baskerville, a typeface based on the types of John Baskerville (1706-1775), an accomplished writing master and printer from Birmingham, England. He was the designer of several types, punchcut by John Handy, which are the basis for the fonts that bear the name Baskerville today. The excellent quality of his printing influenced such famous printers as Didot in France and Bodoni in Italy. His fellow Englishmen imitated his types, and in 1768, Isaac Moore punchcut a version of Baskerville's letterforms for the Fry Foundry. Baskerville produced a masterpiece folio Bible for Cambridge University, and today, his types are considered to be fine representations of eighteenth century rationalism and neoclassicism. This ITC New Baskerville was designed by Matthew Carter and John Quaranda in 1978.

Composed at JTC Imagineering, Santa Maria, CA
Designed by John Taylor-Convery